The Hole in the Wall

Arthur Morrison

The Hole in the Wall

The present edition is a reproduction of previous publication of this classic work. Minor typographical errors may have been corrected without note; however, for an authentic reading experience the spelling, punctuation, and capitalization have been retained from the original text.

ISBN: 978-1-64799-918-6

To
MRS. CHARLES EARDLEY-WILMOT

CONTENTS

CHAPTER I: STEPHEN'S TALE 1
CHAPTER II: IN BLUE GATE 8
CHAPTER III: STEPHEN'S TALE 13
CHAPTER IV: STEPHEN'S TALE 18
CHAPTER V: IN THE HIGHWAY 25
CHAPTER VI: STEPHEN'S TALE 28
CHAPTER VII: STEPHEN'S TALE 33
CHAPTER VIII: STEPHEN'S TALE 40
CHAPTER IX: STEPHEN'S TALE 43
CHAPTER X: STEPHEN'S TALE 46
CHAPTER XI: STEPHEN'S TALE 51
CHAPTER XII: IN THE CLUB-ROOM 58
CHAPTER XIII: STEPHEN'S TALE 64
CHAPTER XIV: STEPHEN'S TALE 69
CHAPTER XV: STEPHEN'S TALE 72
CHAPTER XVI: STEPHEN'S TALE 76
CHAPTER XVII: IN BLUE GATE 82
CHAPTER XVIII: ON THE COP 91
CHAPTER XIX: ON THE COP 94
CHAPTER XX: STEPHEN'S TALE 98
CHAPTER XXI: IN THE BAR-PARLOUR 101
CHAPTER XXII: ON THE COP 105
CHAPTER XXIII: ON THE COP 113
CHAPTER XXIV: ON THE COP 116
CHAPTER XXV: STEPHEN'S TALE 121
CHAPTER XXVI: STEPHEN'S TALE 126
CHAPTER XXVII: IN THE BAR-PARLOUR 130
CHAPTER XXVIII: STEPHEN'S TALE 134
CHAPTER XXIX: STEPHEN'S TALE 139
CHAPTER XXX: STEPHEN'S TALE 141

CHAPTER I
STEPHEN'S TALE

My grandfather was a publican—and a sinner, as you will see. His public-house was the Hole in the Wall, on the river's edge at Wapping; and his sins—all of them that I know of—are recorded in these pages. He was a widower of some small substance, and the Hole in the Wall was not the sum of his resources, for he owned a little wharf on the river Lea. I called him Grandfather Nat, not to distinguish him among a multitude of grandfathers—for indeed I never knew another of my own—but because of affectionate habit; a habit perhaps born of the fact that Nathaniel Kemp was also my father's name. My own is Stephen.

To remember Grandfather Nat is to bethink me of pear-drops. It is possible that that particular sort of sweetstuff is now obsolete, and I cannot remember how many years have passed since last I smelt it; for the pear-drop was a thing that could be smelt farther than seen, and oftener; so that its smell—a rather fulsome, vulgar smell I now believe—is almost as distinct to my imagination while I write as it was to my nose thirty years ago. For pear-drops were an unfailing part of the large bagful of sticky old-fashioned lollipops that my grandfather brought on his visits, stuffed into his overcoat pocket, and hard to get out without a burst and a spill. His custom was invariable, so that I think I must have come to regard the sweets as some natural production of his coat pocket; insomuch that at my mother's funeral my muddled brain scarce realised the full desolation of the circumstances till I discovered that, for the first time in my experience, my grandfather's pocket was void of pear-drops. But with this new bereavement the world seemed empty indeed, and I cried afresh.

Associated in my memory with my grandfather's bag of sweets, almost more than with himself, was the gap in the right hand where the middle finger had been; for it was commonly the maimed hand that hauled out the paper bag, and the gap was plain and singular against the white paper. He had lost the finger at sea, they told me; and as my notion of losing a thing was derived from my Noah's ark, or dropping a marble through a grating, I was long puzzled to guess how anything like that could have happened to a finger. Withal the circumstance fascinated me, and added vastly to

1

the importance and the wonder of my grandfather in my childish eyes.

He was perhaps a little over the middle height, but so broad and so deep of chest and, especially, so long of arm, as to seem squat. He had some grey hair, but it was all below the line of his hat-brim; above that it was as the hair of a young man. So that I was led to reason that colour must be washed out of hair by exposure to the weather; as perhaps in his case it was. I think that his face was almost handsome, in a rough, hard-bitten way, and he was as hairy a man as I ever saw. His short beard was like curled wire; but I can remember that long after I had grown to resent being kissed by women, being no longer a baby, I gladly climbed his knee to kiss my grandfather, though his shaven upper-lip was like a rasp.

In these early days I lived with my mother in a little house of a short row that stood on a quay, in a place that was not exactly a dock, nor a wharf, nor a public thoroughfare; but where people from the dock trying to find a wharf, people from a wharf looking for the dock, and people from the public thoroughfare in anxious search of dock and wharves, used to meet and ask each other questions. It was a detached piece of Blackwall which had got adrift among locks and jetties, and was liable to be cut off from the rest of the world at any moment by the arrival of a ship and the consequent swinging of a bridge, worked by two men at a winch. So that it was a commonplace of my early childhood (though the sight never lost its interest) to observe from a window a ship, passing as it were up the street, warped into dock by the capstans on the quay. And the capstan-songs of the dockmen—Shenandore, Mexico is covered with Snow, Hurrah for the Black Ball Line, and the like—were as much my nursery rhymes as Little Boy Blue and Sing a Song o' Sixpence. These things are done differently nowadays; the cottages on the quay are gone, and the neighbourhood is a smokier place, where the work is done by engines, with no songs.

My father was so much at sea that I remember little of him at all. He was a ship's officer, and at the time I am to tell of he was mate of the brig Juno, owned by Viney and Marr, one of the small shipowning firms that were common enough thirty years ago, though rarer now; the sort of firm that was made by a pushing skipper and an ambitious shipping clerk, beginning with a cheap vessel bought with money raised mainly by pawning the ship. Such concerns often did well, and sometimes grew into great lines; perhaps most of them yielded the partners no more than a comfortable subsistence; and a good few came to grief, or were kept going by questionable practices which have since become illegal—

sometimes in truth by what the law called crime, even then. Viney had been a ship's officer—had indeed served under Grandfather Nat, who was an old skipper. Marr was the business man who had been a clerk. And the firm owned two brigs, the Juno and another; though how much of their value was clear property and how much stood for borrowed money was matter of doubt and disagreement in the conversation of mates and skippers along Thames shore. What nobody disagreed about, however, was that the business was run on skinflint principles, and that the vessels were so badly found, so ill-kept, and so grievously under-manned, that the firm ought to be making money. These things by the way, though they are important to remember. As I was saying, I remember little of my father, because of his long voyages and short spells at home. But my mother is so clear and so kind in my recollection that sometimes I dream of her still, though she died before I was eight.

It was while my father was on a long voyage with the Juno that there came a time when she took me often upon her knee, asking if I should like a little brother or sister to play with; a thing which I demanded to have brought, instantly. There was a fat woman called Mrs. Dann, who appeared in the household and became my enemy. She slept with my mother, and my cot was thrust into another room, where I lay at night and brooded—sometimes wept with jealousy thus to be supplanted; though I drew what consolation I might from the prospect of the promised playmate. Then I could not go near my mother at all, for she was ill, and there was a doctor. And then ... I was told that mother and baby-brother were gone to heaven together; a thing I would not hear of, but fought savagely with Mrs. Dann on the landing, shouting to my mother that she was not to die, for I was coming. And when, wearied with kicking and screaming—for I fought with neighbours as well as with the nurse and the undertaker, conceiving them to be all in league to deprive me of my mother—when at last the woman from next door took me into the bedroom, and I saw the drawn face that could not smile, and my tiny brother that could not play, lying across the dead breast, I so behaved that the good soul with me blubbered aloud; and I had an added grief in the reflection that I had kicked her shins not half an hour before. I have never seen that good woman since; and I am ashamed to write that I cannot even remember her name.

I have no more to say of my mother, and of her funeral only so much as records the least part of my grief. Some of her relations came, whom I cannot distinctly remember seeing at any other time: a group of elderly and hard-featured women, who talked of me as

3

"the child," very much as they might have talked of some troublesome article of baggage; and who turned up their noses at my grandfather: who, for his part, was uneasily respectful, calling each of them "mum" very often. I was not attracted by my mother's relations, and I kept as near my grandfather as possible, feeling a vague fear that some of them might have a design of taking me away. Though indeed none was in the least ambitious of that responsibility.

They were not all women, for there was one quiet little man in their midst, who, when not eating cake or drinking wine, was sucking the bone handle of a woman's umbrella, which he carried with him everywhere, indoors and out. He was in the custody of the largest and grimmest of ladies, whom the others called Aunt Martha. He was so completely in her custody that after some consideration I judged he must be her son; though indeed he seemed very old for that. I now believe him to have been her husband; but I cannot remember to have heard his name, and I cannot invent him a better one than Uncle Martha.

Uncle Martha would have behaved quite well, I am convinced, if he had been left alone, and would have acquitted himself with perfect propriety in all the transactions of the day; but it seemed to be Aunt Martha's immovable belief that he was wholly incapable of any action, even the simplest and most obvious, unless impelled by shoves and jerks. Consequently he was shoved into the mourning carriage—we had two—and jerked into the corner opposite to the one he selected; shoved out—almost on all fours—at the cemetery; and, perceiving him entering the little chapel of his own motion, Aunt Martha overtook him and jerked him in there. This example presently impressed the other ladies with the expediency of shoving Uncle Martha at any convenient opportunity; so that he arrived home with us at last in a severely jostled condition, faithful to the bone-handled umbrella through everything.

Grandfather Nat had been liberal in provision for the funeral party, and the cake and port wine, the gin and water, the tea and the watercress, occupied the visitors for some time; a period illuminated by many moral reflections from a rather fat relation, who was no doubt, like most of the others, an aunt.

"Ah well," said the Fat Aunt, shaking her head, with a deep sigh that suggested repletion; "ah well; it's what we must all come to!"

There had been a deal of other conversation, but I remember this remark because the Fat Aunt had already made it twice.

4

"Ah, indeed," assented another aunt, a thin one; "so we must, sooner or later."

"Yes, yes; as I often say, we're all mortal."

"Yes, indeed!"

"We've all got to be born, an' we've all got to die."

"That's true!"

"Rich an' poor—just the same."

"Ah!"

"In the midst of life we're in the middle of it."

"Ah yes!"

Grandfather Nat, deeply impressed, made haste to refill the Fat Aunt's glass, and to push the cake-dish nearer. Aunt Martha jerked Uncle Martha's elbow toward his glass, which he was neglecting, with a sudden nod and a frown of pointed significance— even command.

"It's a great trial for all of the family, I'm sure," pursued the Fat Aunt, after applications to glass and cake-dish; "but we must bear up. Not that we ain't had trials enough, neither."

"No, indeed," replied Aunt Martha with a snap at my grandfather, as though he were the trial chiefly on her mind; which Grandfather Nat took very humbly, and tried her with watercress.

"Well, she's better off, poor thing," the Fat Aunt went on.

Some began to say "Ah!" again, but Aunt Martha snapped it into "Well, let's hope so!"—in the tone of one convinced that my mother couldn't be much worse off than she had been. From which, and from sundry other remarks among the aunts, I gathered that my mother was held to have hurt the dignity of her family by alliance with Grandfather Nat's. I have never wholly understood why; but I put the family pride down to the traditional wedding of an undoubted auctioneer with Aunt Martha's cousin. So Aunt Martha said "Let's hope so!" and, with another sudden frown and nod, shoved Uncle Martha toward the cake.

"What a blessing the child was took too!" was the Fat Aunt's next observation.

"Ah, that it is!" murmured the chorus. But I was puzzled and shocked to hear such a thing said of my little brother.

"And it's a good job there's only one left."

The chorus agreed again. I began to feel that I had seriously disobliged my mother's relations by not dying too.

"And him a boy; boys can look after themselves." This was a thin aunt's opinion.

"Ah, and that's a blessing," sighed the Fat Aunt; "a great blessing."

"Of course," said Aunt Martha. "And it's not to be expected that his mother's relations can be burdened with him."

"Why, no indeed!" said the Fat Aunt, very decisively.

"I'm sure it wouldn't be poor Ellen's wish to cause more trouble to her family than she has!" And Aunt Martha, with a frown at the watercress, gave Uncle Martha another jolt. It seemed to me that he had really eaten all he wanted, and would rather leave off; and I wondered if she always fed him like that, or if it were only when they were visiting.

"And besides, it 'ud be standing in the child's way," Aunt Martha resumed, "with so many openings as there is in the docks here, quite handy."

Perhaps it was because I was rather dull in the head that day, from one cause and another; at any rate I could think of no other openings in the docks but those between the ships and the jetties, and at the lock-sides, which people sometimes fell into, in the dark; and I gathered a hazy notion that I was expected to make things comfortable by going out and drowning myself.

"Yes, of course it would," said the Fat Aunt.

"It stands to reason," said a thin one.

"Anybody can see that," said the others.

"And many a boy's gone out to work no older."

"Ah, and been members o' Parliament afterwards, too."

The prospect of an entry into Parliament presented so stupefying a contrast with that of an immersion in the dock that for some time the ensuing conversation made little impression on me. On the part of my mother's relations it was mainly a repetition of what had gone before, very much in the same words; and as to my grandfather, he had little to say at all, but expressed himself, so far as he might, by furtive pats on my back; pats increasing in intensity as the talk of the ladies pointed especially and unpleasingly to myself. Till at last the food and drink were all gone. Whereupon the Fat Aunt sighed her last moral sentiment, Uncle Martha was duly shoved out on the quay, and I was left alone with Grandfather Nat.

"Well Stevy, ol' mate," said my grandfather, drawing me on his knee; "us two's left alone; left alone, ol' mate."

I had not cried much that day—scarce at all in fact, since first meeting my grandfather in the passage and discovering his empty pocket—for, as I have said, I was a little dull in the head, and trying hard to think of many things. But now I cried indeed, with my face against my grandfather's shoulder, and there was something of solace in the outburst; and when at last I looked up I saw two bright drops hanging in the wiry tangle of my grandfather's beard, and another lodged in the furrow under one eye.

"'Nough done, Stevy," said my grandfather; "don't cry no more. You'll come home along o' me now, won't ye? An' to-morrow we'll go in the London Dock, where the sugar is."

I looked round the room and considered, as well as my sodden little head would permit. I had never been in the London Dock, which was a wonderful place, as I had gathered from my grandfather's descriptions: a paradise where sugar lay about the very ground in lumps, and where you might eat it if you would, so long as you brought none away. But here was my home, with nobody else to take care of it, and I felt some muddled sense of a new responsibility. "I'm 'fraid I can't leave the place, Gran'fa' Nat," I said, with a dismal shake of the head. "Father might come home, an' he wouldn't know, an'——"

"An' so—an' so you think you've got to stop an' keep house?" my grandfather asked, bending his face down to mine.

The prospect had been oppressing my muzzy faculties all day. If I escaped being taken away, plainly I must keep house, and cook, and buy things and scrub floors, at any rate till my father came home; though it seemed a great deal to undertake alone. So I answered with a nod and a forlorn sniff.

"Good pluck! good pluck!" exclaimed my grandfather, exultantly, clapping his hand twice on my head and rubbing it vigorously. "Stevy, ol' mate, me an' you'll get on capital. I knowed you'd make a plucked 'un. But you won't have to keep house alone jest yet. No. You an' me'll keep house together, Stevy, at the Hole in the Wall. Your father won't be home a while yet; an' I'll settle all about this here place. But Lord! what a pluck for a shaver!" And he brightened wonderfully.

In truth there had been little enough of courage in my poor little body, and Grandfather Nat's words brought me a deal of relief. Beyond the vague terrors of loneliness and responsibility, I had been troubled by the reflection that housekeeping cost money, and I had none. For though my mother's half-pay note had been sent in the regular way to Viney and Marr a week before, there had been neither reply nor return of the paper. The circumstance was unprecedented and unaccountable, though the explanation came before very long.

For the present, however, the difficulty was put aside. I put my hand in my grandfather's, and, the door being locked behind us

7

and the key in his pocket, we went out together, on the quay, over the bridge and into the life that was to be new for us both.

CHAPTER II
IN BLUE GATE

While his mother's relations walked out of Stephen's tale, and left his grandfather in it, the tales of all the world went on, each man hero in his own.

Viney and Marr were owners of the brig Juno, away in tropic seas, with Stephen's father chief mate; and at this time the tale of Viney and Marr had just divided into two, inasmuch as the partners were separated and the firm was at a crisis—the crisis responsible for the withholding of Mrs. Kemp's half-pay. No legal form had dissolved the firm, indeed, and scarce half a mile of streets lay between the two men; but in truth Marr had left his partner with uncommon secrecy and expedition, carrying with him all the loose cash he could get together; and a man need travel a very little way to hide in London. So it was that Mr. Viney, left alone to bear the firm's burdens, was loafing, sometimes about his house in Commercial Road, Stepney, sometimes in the back streets and small public-houses hard by; pondering, no doubt, the matter contained in a paper that had that afternoon stricken the colour from the face of one Crooks, ship-chandler, of Shadwell, and had hardly less disquieted others in related trades. While Marr, for the few days since his flight no more dressed like the business partner in a shipowning concern, nor even like a clerk, but in serge and anklejacks, like a foremast hand, was playing up to his borrowed character by being drunk in Blue Gate.

The Blue Gate is gone now—it went with many places of a history only less black when Ratcliff Highway was put to rout. As you left High Street, Shadwell, for the Highway—they made one thoroughfare—the Blue Gate was on your right, almost opposite an evil lane that led downhill to the New Dock. Blue Gate Fields, it was more fully called, though there was as little of a field as of a gate, blue or other, about the place, which was a street, narrow, foul and forbidding, leading up to Back Lane. It was a bad and a dangerous place, the worst in all that neighbourhood: worse than Frederick Street—worse than Tiger Bay. The sailor once brought to anchor in

8

Blue Gate was lucky to get out with clothes to cover him—lucky if he saved no more than his life. Yet sailors were there in plenty, hilarious, shouting, drunk and drugged. Horrible draggled women pawed them over for whatever their pockets might yield, and murderous ruffians were ready at hand whenever a knock on the head could solve a difficulty.

Front doors stood ever open in the Blue Gate, and some houses had no front doors at all. At the top of one of the grimy flights of stairs thus made accessible from the street, was a noisy and ill-smelling room; noisy because of the company it held; ill-smelling partly because of their tobacco, but chiefly because of the tobacco and the liquor of many that had been there before, and because of the aged foulness of the whole building. There were five in the room, four men and a woman. One of the men was Marr, though for the present he was not using that name. He was noticeable amid the group, being cleaner than the rest, fair-haired, and dressed like a sailor ashore, though he lacked the sunburn that was proper to the character. But sailor or none, there he sat where many had sat before him, a piece of the familiar prey of Blue Gate, babbling drunk and reasonless. The others were watchfully sober enough, albeit with a great pretence of jollity; they had drunk level with the babbler, but had been careful to water his drink with gin. As for him, he swayed and lolled, sometimes on the table before him, sometimes on the shoulder of the woman at his side. She was no beauty, with her coarse features, dull eyes, and tousled hair, her thick voice and her rusty finery; but indeed she was the least repulsive of that foul company.

On the victim's opposite side sat a large-framed bony fellow, with a thin, unhealthy face that seemed to belong to some other body, and dress that proclaimed him long-shore ruffian. The woman called him Dan, and nods and winks passed between the two, over the drooping head between them. Next Dan was an ugly rascal with a broken nose; singular in that place, as bearing in his dress none of the marks of waterside habits, crimpery and the Highway, but seeming rather the commonplace town rat of Shoreditch or Whitechapel. And, last, a blind fiddler sat in a corner, fiddling a flourish from time to time, roaring with foul jest, and roiling his single white eye upward.

"No, I won'av another," the fair-haired man said, staring about him with uncertain eyes. "Got bishness 'tend to. I say, wha' pubsh this? 'Tain' Brown Bear, ish't? Ish't Brown Bear?"

"No, you silly," the woman answered playfully. "'Tain't the Brown Bear; you've come 'ome along of us."

9

"O! Come home—come home.... I shay—this won' do! Mus'n' go 'ome yet—get collared y'know!" This with an owlish wink at the bottle before him.

Dan and the woman exchanged a quick look; plainly something had gone before that gave the words significance. "No," Marr went on, "mus'n' go 'ome. I'm sailor man jus' 'shore from brig Juno in from Barbadoes.... No, not Juno, course not. Dunno Juno. 'Tain' Juno. D'year? 'Tain' Juno, ye know, my ship. Never heard o' Juno. Mine's 'nother ship.... I say, wha'sh name my ship?"

"You're a rum sailor-man," said Dan, "not to know the name of your own ship ten minutes together. Why, you've told us about four different names a'ready."

The sham seaman chuckled feebly.

"Why, I don't believe you're a sailor at all, mate," the woman remarked, still playfully. "You've just bin a-kiddin' of us fine!"

The chuckle persisted, and turned to a stupid grin. "Ha, ha! Ha, ha! Have it y'r own way." This with a clumsily stealthy grope at the breast pocket—a movement that the others had seen before, and remembered. "Have it y'r own way. But I say; I say, y'know"— suddenly serious—"you're all right, ain't you? Eh? All right, you know, eh? I s-say—I hope you're—orright?"

"Awright, mate? Course we are!" And Dan clapped him cordially on the shoulder.

"Awright, mate?" shouted the blind man, his white eye rolling and blinking horribly at the ceiling. "Right as ninepence! An' a 'a'penny over, damme!"

"We're awright," growled the broken-nosed man, thickly.

"We don't tell no secrets," said the woman.

"Thash all very well, but I was talkin' about the Juno, y'know. Was'n I talkin' about Juno?" A look of sleepy alarm was on the fair man's face as he turned his eyes from one to another.

"Ay, that's so," answered the fellow at his side. "Brig Juno in from Barbadoes."

"Ah! Thash where you're wrong; she ain't in—see?" Marr wagged his head, and leered the profoundest sagacity. "She ain't in. What's more, 'ow d'you know she ever will come in, eh? 'Ow d'ye know that? Thash one for ye, ole f'ler! Whar'll ye bet me she ever gets as far as—but I say, I say; I say, y'know, you're all right, ain't you? Qui' sure you're orrigh'?"

There was a new and a longer chorus of reassurance, which Dan at last ended with: "Go on; the Juno ain't ever to come back; is that it?"

Marr turned and stared fishily at him for some seconds.

"Wha'rr you mean?" he demanded, at length, with a drivelling assumption of dignity. "Wha'rr you mean? N-never come back? Nishe remark make 'spectable shipowner! Whassor' firm you take us for, eh?"

The blind fiddler stopped midway in a flourish and pursed his lips silently. Dan looked quickly at the fiddler, and as quickly back at the drunken man. Marr's attitude and the turn of his head being favourable, the woman quietly detached his watch.

"Whassor' firm you take us for?" he repeated. "D'ye think 'cause we're—'cause I come here—'cause I come 'ere an'——" he stopped foolishly, and tailed off into nothing, smiling uneasily at one and another.

The woman held up the watch behind him—a silver hunter, engraved with Marr's chief initial—a noticeably large letter M. Dan saw it, shook his head and frowned, pointed and tapped his own breast pocket, all in a moment. And presently the woman slipped the watch back into the pocket it came from.

"'Ere, 'ave another drink," said Dan hospitably. "'Ave another all round for the last, 'fore the fiddler goes. 'Ere y'are, George, reach out."

"Eh?" ejaculated the fiddler. "Eh? I ain't goin'! Didn't the genelman ask me to come along? Come, I'll give y' a toon. I'll give y' a chant as 'll make yer 'air curl!"

"Take your drink, George," Dan insisted, "we don't want our 'air curled."

The fiddler groped for and took the drink, swallowed it, and twangled the fiddle-strings. "Will y'ave Black Jack?" he asked.

"No," Dan answered with a rising voice. "We won't 'ave Black Jack, an' what's more we won't 'ave Blind George, see? You cut your lucky, soon as ye like!"

"Awright, awright, cap'en," the fiddler remonstrated, rising reluctantly. "You're 'ard on a pore blind bloke, damme. Ain't I to get nothin' out o' this 'ere? I ask ye fair, didn't the genelman tell me to come along?"

Marr, ducking and lolling over the table, here looked up and said, "Whassup? Fiddler won' go? Gi'm twopence an' kick'm downstairs. 'Ere y'are!" and he pulled out some small change between his fingers, and spilt it on the table.

Dan and the broken-nosed man gathered it up and thrust it into the blind man's hand. "This ain't the straight game," he protested, in a hoarse whisper, as they pushed him through the doorway. "I want my reg'lars out o' that lot. D'ye 'ear? I want my reg'lars!"

11

But they shut the door on him, whereupon he broke into a torrent of curses on the landing; and presently, having descended several of the stairs, reached back to let drive a thump at the door with his stick; and so went off swearing into the street.

Marr sniggered feebly. "Chucked out fiddler," he said. "Whash we do now? I won'ave any more drink. I 'ad 'nough.... Think I'll be gett'n' along.... Here, what you after, eh?"

He clapped his hand again to his breast pocket, and turned suspiciously on the woman. "You keep y'r hands off," he said. "Wha' wan' my pocket?"

"Awright, mate," the woman answered placidly. "I ain't a touchin' yer pockets. Why, look there—yer watchguard's 'angin'; you'll drop that presently an' say it's me, I s'pose!"

"You'd better get away from the genelman if you can't behave yourself civil," interposed Dan, pushing the woman aside and getting between them. "'Ere, mate, you got to 'ave another drink along o' me. I'll turn her out arter the fiddler, if she ain't civil."

"I won'ave another drink," said Marr, thickly, struggling unsteadily to his feet and dropping back instantly to his chair. "I won'avanother."

"We'll see about that," replied Dan. "'Ere, you get out," he went on, addressing the woman as he hauled her up by the shoulders. "You get out; we're goin' to be comf'table together, us two an' 'im. Out ye go!" He thrust her toward the door and opened it. "I'm sick o' foolin' about," he added in an angry undertone; "quick's the word."

"O no, Dan—don't," the woman pleaded, whispering on the landing. "Not that way! Not again! I'll get it from him easy in a minute! Don't do it, Dan!"

"Shut yer mouth! I ain't askin' you. You shove off a bit."

"Don't, Dan!"

But the door was shut.

"I tell ye I won'avanother!" came Marr's voice from within.

The woman went down the stairs, her gross face drawn as though she wept, though her eyes were dry. At the door she looked back with something like a shudder, and then turned her steps down the street.

The two partners in Viney and Marr were separated indeed; but now it was by something more than half a mile of streets.

CHAPTER III
STEPHEN'S TALE

I had never been home with Grandfather Nat before. I fancy that some scruples of my mother's, in the matter of the neighbourhood and the character of the company to be seen and heard at the Hole in the Wall, had hitherto kept me from the house, and even from the sugary elysium of the London Dock. Now I was going there at last, and something of eager anticipation overcame the sorrow of the day.

We went in an omnibus, which we left in Commercial Road. Here my grandfather took order to repair my disappointment in the matter of pear-drops; and we left the shop with such a bagful that it would not go into the accustomed pocket at all. A little way from this shop, and on the opposite side of the way, stood a house which my mother had more than once pointed out to me already; and as we came abreast of it now, Grandfather Nat pointed it out also. "Know who lives there, Stevy?" he asked.

"Yes," I said; "Mr. Viney, that father's ship belongs to."

There was a man sitting on the stone baluster by the landing of the front steps, having apparently just desisted from knocking at the door. He was pale and agitated, and he slapped his leg distractedly with a folded paper.

"Why," said my grandfather, "that's Crooks, the ship-chandler. He looks bad; wonder what's up?"

With that the door opened, and a servant-girl, in bonnet and shawl, emerged with her box, lifting and dragging it as best she might. The man rose and spoke to her, and I supposed that he was about to help. But at her answer he sank back on the balustrade, and she hauled the box to the pavement by herself. The man looked worse than ever, now, and he moved his head from side to side; so that it struck me that it might be that his mother also was dead; perhaps to-day; and at the thought all the flavour went from the pear-drop in my mouth.

We turned up a narrow street which led us to a part where the river plainly was nearer at every step; for well I knew the curious smell that grew as we went, and that had in it something of tar, something of rope and junk, something of ships' stores, and much of a blend of unknown outlandish merchandise. We met sailors, some with parrots and accordions, and many with undecided legs; and we

13

saw more of the hang-dog fellows who were not sailors, though they dressed in the same way, and got an inactive living out of sailors, somehow. They leaned on posts, they lurked in foul entries, they sat on sills, smoking; and often one would accost and hang to a passing sailor, with a grinning, trumped-up cordiality that offended and repelled me, child as I was. And there were big, coarse women, with flaring clothes, and hair that shone with grease; though for them I had but a certain wonder; as for why they all seemed to live near the docks; why they all grew so stout; and why they never wore bonnets.

As we went where the street grew fouler and more crooked, and where dark entries and many turnings gave evidence of the complication of courts and alleys about us, we heard a hoarse voice crooning a stave of a sea-song, with the low scrape of a fiddle striking in here and there, as it were at random. And presently there turned a corner ahead and faced toward us a blind man, with his fiddle held low against his chest, and his face lifted upward, a little aside. He checked at the corner to hit the wall a couple of taps with the stick that hung from his wrist, and called aloud, with fouler words than I can remember or could print: "Now then, damn ye! Ain't there ne'er a Christian sailor-man as wants a toon o' George? Who'll 'ave a toon o' George? Ain't ye got no money, damn ye? Not a brown for pore blind George? What a dirty mean lot it is! Who'll 'ave a 'ornpipe? Who'll 'ave a song o' pore George?... O damn y' all!"

And so, with a mutter and another tap of the stick, he came creeping along, six inches at a step, the stick dangling loose again, and the bow scraping the strings to the song:—

Fire on the fore-top, fire on the bow, Fire on the main-deck, fire down below! Fire! fire! fire down below! Fetch a bucket o' water; fire down below!

The man's right eye was closed, but the left was horribly wide and white and rolling, and it quite unpleasantly reminded me of a large china marble that lay at that moment at the bottom of my breeches pocket, under some uniform buttons, a key you could whistle on, a brass knob from a fender, and a tangle of string. So much indeed was I possessed with this uncomfortable resemblance in later weeks, when I had seen Blind George often, and knew more of him, that at last I had no choice but to fling the marble into the river; though indeed it was something of a rarity in marbles, and worth four "alleys" as big as itself.

My grandfather stopped his talk as we drew within earshot of the fiddler; but blind men's ears are keen beyond the common. The bow dropped from the fiddle, and Blind George sang out cheerily: "Why, 'ere comes Cap'en Nat, 'ome from the funeral; and got 'is little

14

grandson what 'e's goin' to take care of an' bring up so moral in 'is celebrated 'ouse o' call!" All to my extreme amazement: for what should this strange blind man know of me, or of my mother's funeral?

Grandfather Nat seemed a little angry. "Well, well," he said, "your ears are sharp, Blind George; they learn a lot as ain't your business. If your eyes was as good as your ears you'd ha' had your head broke 'fore this—a dozen times!"

"If my eyes was as good as my ears, Cap'en Nat Kemp," the other retorted, "there's many as wouldn't find it so easy to talk o' breakin' my 'ed. Other people's business! Lord! I know enough to 'ang some of 'em, that's what I know! I could tell you some o' your business if I liked,—some as you don't know yourself. Look 'ere! You bin to a funeral. Well, it ain't the last funeral as 'll be wanted in your family; see? The kid's mother's gone; don't you be too sure 'is father's safe! I bin along o' some one you know, an' 'e don't look like lastin' for ever, 'e don't; 'e ain't in 'ealthy company."

Grandfather Nat twitched my sleeve, and we walked on.

"Awright!" the blind man called after us, in his tone of affable ferocity. "Awright, go along! You'll see things, some day, near as well as I can, what's blind!"

"That's a bad fellow, Stevy," Grandfather Nat said, as we heard the fiddle and the song begin again. "Don't you listen to neither his talk nor his songs. Somehow it don't seem nat'ral to see a blind man such a bad 'un. But a bad 'un he is, up an' down."

I asked how he came to know about the funeral, and especially about my coming to Wapping—a thing I had only learned of myself an hour before. My grandfather said that he had probably learned of the funeral from somebody who had been at the Hole in the Wall during the day, and had asked the reason of the landlord's absence; and as to myself, he had heard my step, and guessed its meaning instantly. "He's a keen sharp rascal, Stevy, an' he makes out all of parties' business he can. He knew your father was away, an' he jumped the whole thing at once. That's his way. But I don't stand him; he don't corne into my house barrin' he comes a customer, which I can't help."

Of the meaning of the blind man's talk I understood little. But he shocked me with a sense of insult, and more with one of surprise. For I had entertained a belief, born of Sunday-school stories, that blindness produced saintly piety—unless it were the piety that caused the blindness—and that in any case a virtuous meekness was an essential condition of the affliction. So I walked in doubt and cogitation.

15

And so, after a dive down a narrower street than any we had yet traversed (it could scarce be dirtier), and a twist through a steep and serpentine alley, we came, as it grew dusk, to the Hole in the Wall. Of odd-looking riverside inns I can remember plenty, but never, before or since, have I beheld an odder than this of Grandfather Nat's. It was wooden and clap-boarded, and, like others of its sort, it was everywhere larger at top than at bottom. But the Hole in the Wall was not only top-heavy, but also most alarmingly lopsided. By its side, and half under it, lay a narrow passage, through which one saw a strip of the river and its many craft, and the passage ended in Hole-in-the-Wall Stairs. All of the house that was above the ground floor on this side rested on a row of posts, which stood near the middle of the passage; and the burden of these posts, twisted, wavy, bulging, and shapeless, hung still more toward the opposite building; while the farther side, bounded by a later brick house, was vertical, as though a great wedge, point downward, had been cut away to permit the rise of the newer wall. And the effect was as of a reeling and toppling of the whole construction away from its neighbour, and an imminent downfall into the passage. And when, later, I examined the side looking across the river, supported on piles, and bulging and toppling over them also, I decided that what kept the Hole in the Wall from crashing into the passage was nothing but its countervailing inclination to tumble into the river.

Painted large over the boards of the front, whose lapped edges gave the letters ragged outlines, were the words THE HOLE IN THE WALL; and below, a little smaller, NATHANIEL KEMP. I felt a certain pride, I think, in the importance thus given the family name, and my esteem of my grandfather increased proportionably with the size of the letters.

There was a great noise within, and Grandfather Nat, with a quick look toward the entrance, grunted angrily. But we passed up the passage and entered by a private door under the posts. This door opened directly into the bar parlour, the floor whereof was two steps below the level of the outer paving; and the size whereof was about thrice that of a sentry-box.

The din of a quarrel and a scuffle came from the bar, and my grandfather, thrusting me into a corner, and giving me his hat, ran out with a roar like that of a wild beast. At the sound the quarrel hushed in its height. "What's this?" my grandfather blared, with a thump on the counter that made the pots jump. "What sort of a row's this in my house? Damme, I'll break y' in halves, every mother's son of ye!"

I peeped through the glass partition, and saw, first, the back of the potman's head (for the bar-floor took another drop) and beyond that and the row of beer-pulls, a group of rough, hulking men, one with blood on his face, and all with an odd look of sulky guilt.

"Out you go!" pursued Grandfather Nat, "every swab o' ye! Can't leave the place not even to go to—not for nothin', without a row like this, givin' the house a bad name! Go on, Jim Crute! Unless I'm to chuck ye!"

The men had begun filing out awkwardly, with nothing but here and there: "Awright, guv'nor"—"Awright, cap'en." "Goin', ain't I?" and the like. But one big ruffian lagged behind, scowling and murmuring rebelliously.

In a flash Grandfather Nat was through the counter-wicket. With a dart of his long left arm he had gripped the fellow's ear and spun him round with a wrench that I thought had torn the ear from the head; and in the same moment had caught him by the opposite wrist, so as to stretch the man's extended arm, elbow backward, across his own great chest; a posture in which the backward pull against the elbow joint brought a yell of agony from the victim. Only a man with extraordinarily long arms could have done the thing exactly like that. The movement was so savagely sudden that my grandfather had kicked open the door and flung Jim Crute headlong into the street ere I quite understood it; when there came a check in my throat and tears in my eyes to see the man so cruelly handled.

Grandfather Nat stood a moment at the door, but it seemed that his customer was quelled effectually, for presently he turned inward again, with such a grim scowl as I had never seen before. And at that a queer head appeared just above the counter—I had supposed the bar to be wholly cleared—and a very weak and rather womanish voice said, in tones of over-inflected indignation: "Serve 'em right, Cap'en Kemp, I'm sure. Lot o' impudent vagabones! Ought to be ashamed o' theirselves, that they ought. Pity every 'ouse ain't kep' as strict as this one is, that's what I say!"

And the queer head looked round the vacant bar with an air of virtuous defiance, as though anxious to meet the eye of any so bold as to contradict.

It was anything but a clean face on the head, and it was overshadowed by a very greasy wideawake hat. Grubbiness and unhealthy redness contended for mastery in the features, of which the nose was the most surprising, wide and bulbous and knobbed all over; so that ever afterward, in any attempt to look Mr. Cripps in the face, I found myself wholly disregarding his eyes, and fixing a

17

fascinated gaze on his nose; and I could never recall his face to memory as I recalled another, but always as a Nose, garnished with a fringe of inferior features. The face had been shaved—apparently about a week before; and by the sides hung long hair, dirtier to look at than the rest of the apparition.

My grandfather gave no more than a glance in the direction of this little man, passed the counter and re-joined me, pulling off his coat as he came. Something of my tingling eyes and screwed mouth was visible, I suppose, for he stooped as he rolled up his shirt-sleeves and said: "Why, Stevy boy, what's amiss?"

"You—you—hurt the man's ear," I said, with a choke and a sniff; for till then Grandfather Nat had seemed to me the kindest man in the world.

Grandfather Nat looked mightily astonished. He left his shirt-sleeve where it was, and thrust his fingers up in his hair behind, through the grey and out at the brown on top. "What?" he said. "Hurt 'im? Hurt 'im? Why, s'pose I did? He ain't a friend o' yours, is he, young 'un?"

I shook my head and blinked. There was a gleam of amusement in my grandfather's grim face as he sat in a chair and took me between his knees. "Hurt 'im?" he repeated. "Why, Lord love ye, I'd get hurt if I didn't hurt some of 'em, now an' then. They're a rough lot—a bitter bad lot round here, an' it's hurt or be hurt with them, Stevy. I got to frighten 'em, my boy—an' I do it, too."

I was passing my fingers to and fro in the matted hair on my grandfather's arm, and thinking. He seemed a very terrible man now, and perhaps something of a hero; for, young as I was, I was a boy. So presently I said, "Did you ever kill a man, Gran'fa' Nat?"

CHAPTER IV
STEPHEN'S TALE

Many small matters of my first few hours at the Hole in the Wall were impressed on me by later events. In particular I remember the innocent curiosity with which I asked: "Did you ever kill a man, Gran'fa' Nat?"

There was a twitch and a frown on my grandfather's face, and he sat back as one at a moment's disadvantage. I thought that perhaps he was trying to remember. But he only said, gruffly, and with a quick sound like a snort: "Very nigh killed myself once or twice, Stevy, in my time," and rose hastily from his chair to reach a picture of a ship that was standing on a shelf. "There," he said, "that's a new 'un, just done; pretty picter, ain't it? An' that there," pointing to another hanging on the wall, "that's the Juno, what your father's on now."

I had noticed that the walls, both of the bar and of the bar-parlour, were plentifully hung with paintings of ships; ships becalmed, ships in full sail, ships under bare spars; all with painful blue skies over them, and very even-waved seas beneath; and ships in storms, with torn sails, pursued by rumbustious piles of sooty cloud, and pelted with lengths of scarlet lightning. I fear I should not have recognised my father's ship without help, but that was probably because I had only seen it, months before, lying in dock, battered and dingy, with a confusion of casks and bales about the deck, and naked yards dangling above; whereas in the picture (which was a mile too small for the brig) it was booming along under a flatulent mountain of clean white sail, and bulwarks and deck-fittings were gay with lively and diversified colour.

I said something about its being a fine ship, or a fine picture, and that there were a lot of them.

"Ah," he said, "they do mount up, one arter another. It's one gentleman as did 'em all—him out in the bar now, with the long hair. Sometimes I think I'd rather a-had money; but it's a talent, that's what it is!"

The artist beyond the outer bar had been talking to the potman. Now he coughed and said: "Ha—um! Cap'en Kemp, sir! Cap'en Kemp! No doubt as you've 'eard the noos to-day?"

"No," said Grandfather Nat, finishing the rolling of his shirt-sleeves as he stepped down into the bar; "not as I know on. What is it?"

"Not about Viney and Marr?"

"No. What about 'em?"

Mr. Cripps rose on his toes with the importance of his information, and his eyes widened to a moment's rivalry with his nose. "Gone wrong," he said, in a shrill whisper that was as loud as his natural voice. "Gone wrong. Unsolvent. Cracked up. Broke. Busted, in a common way o' speakin'." And he gave a violent nod with each synonym.

"No," said Grandfather Nat; "surely not Viney and Marr?"

19

"Fact, Cap'en; I can assure you, on 'igh a'thority. It's what I might call the universal topic in neighbourin' circles, an' a gen'ral subjick o' local discussion. You'd 'a 'eard it 'fore this if you'd bin at 'ome."

My grandfather whistled, and rested a hand on a beer-pull.

"Not a stiver for nobody, they say," Mr. Cripps pursued, "not till they can sell the wessels. What there was loose Marr's bolted with; or, as you might put it, absconded; absconded with the proceeds. An' gone abroad, it's said."

"I see the servant gal bringin' out her box from Viney's just now," said Grandfather Nat. "An' Crooks the ship-chandler was on the steps, very white in the gills, with a paper. Well, well! An' you say Marr's bolted?"

"Absconded, Cap'en Kemp; absconded with the proceeds; 'opped the twig. Viney says 'e's robbed 'im as well as the creditors, but I 'ear some o' the creditors' observation is 'gammon.' An' they say the wessels is pawned up to their r'yals. Up to their r'yals!"

"Well," commented my grandfather, "I wouldn't ha' thought it. The Juno was that badly found, an' they did everything that cheap, I thought they made money hand over fist."

"Flyin' too 'igh, Cap'en Kemp, flyin' too 'igh. You knowed Viney long 'fore 'e elevated hisself into a owner, didn't you? What was he then? Why, 'e was your mate one voy'ge, wasn't he?"

"Ay, an' more."

"So I've 'eard tell. Well, arter that surely 'e was flyin' too 'igh! An' now Marr's absconded with the proceeds!"

The talk in the bar went on, being almost entirely the talk of Mr. Cripps; who valued himself on the unwonted importance his news gave him, and aimed at increasing it by saying the same thing a great many times; by saying it, too, when he could, in terms and phrases that had a strong flavour of the Sunday paper. But as for me, I soon ceased to hear, for I discovered something of greater interest on the shelf that skirted the bar-parlour. It was a little model of a ship in a glass case, and it was a great marvel to me, with all its standing and running rigging complete, and a most ingenious and tumultuous sea about it, made of stiff calico cockled up into lumps and ridges, and painted the proper colour. Much better than either of the two we had at home, for these latter were only half-models, each nothing but one-half of a little ship split from stem to stern, and stuck against a board, on which were painted sky, clouds, seagulls, and (in one case) a lighthouse; an exasperating make-believe that had been my continual disappointment.

But this was altogether so charming and delightful and real, and the little hatches and cuddy-houses so thrilled my fancy, that I resolved to beg of my grandfather to let me call the model my own, and sometimes have the glass case off. So I was absorbed while the conversation in the bar ranged from the ships and their owners to my father, and from him to me; as was plain when my grandfather called me.

"Here he is," said my grandfather, with a deal of pride in his voice, putting his foot on a stool and lifting me on his knee. "Here he is, an' a plucked 'un; ain't ye, Stevy?" He rubbed his hand over my head, as he was fond of doing. "Plucked? Ah! Why, he was agoin' to keep house all by hisself, with all the pluck in life, till his father come home! Warn't ye, Stevy boy? But he's come along o' me instead, an' him an' me's goin' to keep the Hole in the Wall together, ain't we? Pardners: eh, Stevy?"

I think I never afterwards saw my grandfather talking so familiarly with his customers. I perceived now that there was another in the bar in addition to Mr. Cripps; a pale, quiet, and rather ragged man who sat in an obscure corner with an untouched glass of liquor by him.

"Come," said my grandfather, "have one with me, Mr. Cripps, an' drink the new pardner's health. What is it? An' you—you drink up too, an' have another." This last order Grandfather Nat flung at the man in the corner, just in the tones in which I had heard a skipper on a ship tell a man to "get forrard lively" with a rope fender, opposite our quay at Blackwall.

"I'm sure 'ere's wishin' the young master every 'ealth an' 'appiness," said Mr. Cripps, beaming on me with a grin that rather frightened than pleased me, it twisted the nose so. "Every 'ealth and 'appiness, I'm sure!"

The pale man in the corner only looked up quickly, as if fearful of obtruding himself, gulped the drink that had been standing by him, and receiving another, put it down untasted where the first had stood.

"That ain't drinkin' a health," said my grandfather, angrily. "There—that's it!" and he pointed to the new drink with the hand that held his own.

The pale man lifted it hurriedly, stood up, looked at me and said something indistinct, gulped the liquor and returned the glass to the counter; whereupon the potman, without orders, instantly refilled it, and the man carried it back to his corner and put it down beside him, as before.

I began to wonder if the pale man suffered from some complaint that made it dangerous to leave him without a drink close at hand, ready to be swallowed at a moment's notice. But Mr. Cripps blinked, first at his own glass and then at the pale man's; and I fancy he thought himself unfairly treated.

Howbeit his affability was unconquerable. He grinned and snapped his fingers playfully at me, provoking my secret indignation; since that was what people did to please babies.

"An' a pretty young gent 'e is too," said Mr. Cripps, "of considerable personal attractions. Goin' to bring 'im up to the trade, I s'pose, Cap'en Kemp?"

"Why, no," said Grandfather Nat, with some dignity. "No. Something better than that, I'm hopin'. Pardners is all very well for a bit, but Stevy's goin' to be a cut above his poor old gran'father, if I can do it. Eh, boy?" He rubbed my head again, and I was too shy, sitting there in the bar, to answer. "Eh, boy? Boardin' school an' a gentleman's job for this one, if the old man has his way."

Mr. Cripps shook his head sagaciously, and could plainly see that I was cut out for a statesman. He also lifted his empty glass, looked at it abstractedly, and put it down again. Nothing coming of this, he complimented my personal appearance once more, and thought that my portrait should certainly be painted, as a memorial in my future days of greatness.

This notion seemed to strike my grandfather rather favourably, and he forthwith consulted a slate which dangled by a string; during his contemplation of which, with its long rows of strokes, Mr. Cripps betrayed a certain anxious discomfort. "Well," said Grandfather Nat at length, "you are pretty deep in, you know, an' it might as well be that as anything else. But what about that sign? Ain't I ever goin' to get that?"

Mr. Cripps knitted his brows and his nose, turned up his eyes and shook his head. "It ain't come to me yet, Cap'en Kemp," he said; "not yet. I'm still waiting for what you might call an inspiration. But when it comes, Cap'en Kemp—when it comes! Ah! you'll 'ave a sign then! Sich a sign! You'll 'ave sich a sign as'll attract the 'ole artistic feelin' of Wapping an' surroundin' districks of the metropolis, I assure you. An' the signs on the other 'ouses—phoo!" Mr. Cripps made a sweep of the hand, which I took to indicate generally that all other publicans, overwhelmed with humiliation, would have no choice but straightway to tear down their own signs and bury them.

"Umph! but meanwhile I haven't got one at all," objected Grandfather Nat; "an' they have."

"Ah, yes, sir—some sort o' signs. But done by mere jobbers, and poor enough too. My hart, Cap'en Kemp—I respect my hart, an' I don't rush at a job like that. It wants conception, sir, a job like

22

that—conception. The common sort o' sign's easy enough. You go at it, an' you do it or hexicute it, an' when it's done or hexicuted—why there it is. A ship, maybe, or a crown, or a Turk's 'ed or three cats an' a fryin' pan. Simple enough—no plannin', no composition, no invention. But a 'ole in a wall, Cap'en Kemp—it takes a hartist to make a picter o' that; an' it takes study, an' meditation, an' invention!"

"Simplest thing o' the lot," said Captain Nat. "A wall, an' a hole in it. Simplest thing o' the lot!"

"As you observe, Cap'en Kemp, it may seem simple enough; that's because you're thinkin' o' subjick, instead o' treatment. A common jobber, if you'll excuse my sayin' it, 'ud look at it just in that light—a wall with a 'ole in it, an' 'e'd give it you, an' p'rhaps you'd be satisfied with it. But I soar 'igher, sir, 'igher. What I shall give you'll be a 'ole in the wall to charm the heye and delight the intelleck, sir. A dramatic 'ole in the wall, sir, a hepic 'ole in the wall; a 'ole in the wall as will elevate the mind and stimilate the noblest instinks of the be'older. Cap'en Kemp, I don't 'esitate to say that my 'ole in the wall, when you get it, will be—ah! it'll be the moral palladium of Wapping!"

"When I get it," my grandfather replied with a chuckle, "anything might happen without surprisin' me. I think p'rhaps I might be so startled as to forget the bit you've had on account, an' pay full cash."

Mr. Cripps's eyes brightened at the hint. "You're always very 'andsome in matters o' business, Cap'en Kemp," he said, "an' I always say so. Which reminds me, speakin' of 'andsome things. This morning goin' to see my friend as keeps the mortuary, I see as 'andsome a bit o' panel for to paint a sign as ever I come across. A lovely bit o' stuff to be sure—enough to stimulate anybody's artistic invention to look at it, that it was. Not dear neither—particular moderate in fact. I'm afraid it may be gone now; but if I'd 'a 'ad the money——"

A noise of trampling and singing without neared the door, and with a bang and a stagger a party of fresh customers burst in and swept Mr. Cripps out of his exposition. Two were sun-browned sailors, shouting and jovial, but the rest, men and women, sober and villainous in their mock jollity, were land-sharks plain to see. The foremost sailor drove against Mr. Cripps, and having almost knocked him down, took him by the shoulders and involved him in his flounderings; apologising, meanwhile, at the top of his voice, and demanding to know what Mr. Cripps would drink. Whereupon

23

Grandfather Nat sent me back to the bar-parlour and the little ship, and addressed himself to business and the order of the bar.

And so he was occupied for the most of the evening. Sometimes he sat with me and taught me the spars and rigging of the model, sometimes I peeped through the glass at the business of the house. The bar remained pretty full throughout the evening, in its main part, and my grandfather ruled its frequenters with a strong voice and an iron hand.

But there was one little space partitioned off, as it might be for the better company: which space was nearly always empty. Into this quieter compartment I saw a man come, rather late in the evening, furtive and a little flustered. He was an ugly ruffian with a broken nose; and he was noticeable as being the one man I had seen in my grandfather's house who had no marks of seafaring or riverside life about him, but seemed merely an ordinary London blackguard from some unmaritime neighbourhood. He beckoned silently to Grandfather Nat, who walked across and conferred with him. Presently my grandfather left the counter and came into the bar-parlour. He had something in his closed hand, which he carried to the lamp to examine, so that I could see it was a silver watch; while the furtive man waited expectantly in the little compartment. The watch interested me, for the inward part swung clean out from the case, and hung by a single hinge, in a way I had never seen before. I noticed, also, that a large capital letter M was engraved on the back.

Grandfather Nat shut the watch and strode into the bar.

"Here you are," he said aloud, handing it to the broken-nosed man. "Here you are. It seems all right—good enough watch, I should say."

The man was plainly disconcerted—frightened, indeed—by this public observation; and answered with an eager whisper.

"What?" my grandfather replied, louder than ever; "want me to buy it? Not me. This ain't a pawnshop. I don't want a watch; an' if I did, how do I know where you got it?"

Much discomposed by this rebuff, the fellow hurried off. Whereupon I was surprised to see the pale man rise from the corner of the bar, put his drink, still untasted, in a safe place on the counter, beyond the edge of the partition, and hurry out also. Cogitating this matter in my grandfather's arm-chair, presently I fell asleep.

What woke me at length was the loud voice of Grandfather Nat, and I found that it was late, and he was clearing the bar before shutting up. I rubbed my eyes and looked out, and was interested to see that the pale man had come back, and was now swallowing his

24

drink at last before going out after the rest. Whereat I turned again, drowsily enough, to the model ship.

But a little later, when Grandfather Nat and I were at supper in the bar-parlour, and I was dropping to sleep again, I was amazed to see my grandfather pull the broken-nosed man's watch out of his pocket and put it in a tin cash-box. At that I rubbed my eyes, and opened them so wide on the cash-box, that Grandfather Nat said, "Hullo, Stevy! Woke up with a jump? Time you was in bed."

CHAPTER V

IN THE HIGHWAY

The Hole in the Wall being closed, its customers went their several ways; the sailors, shouting and singing, drifting off with their retinue along Wapping Wall toward Ratcliff; Mr. Cripps, fuller than usual of free drinks—for the sailors had come a long voyage and were proportionally liberal—scuffling off, steadily enough, on the way that led to Limehouse; for Mr. Cripps had drunk too much and too long ever to be noticeably drunk. And last of all, when the most undecided of the stragglers from Captain Nat Kemp's bar had vanished one way or another, the pale, quiet man moved out from the shadow and went in the wake of the noisy sailors.

The night was dark, and the streets. The lamps were few and feeble, and angles, alleys and entries were shapes of blackness that seemed more solid than the walls about them. But instead of the silence that consorts with gloom, the air was racked with human sounds; sounds of quarrels, scuffles, and brawls, far and near, breaking out fitfully amid the general buzz and whoop of discordant singing that came from all Wapping and Ratcliff where revellers rolled into the open.

A stone's throw on the pale man's way was a swing bridge with a lock by its side, spanning the channel that joined two dock-basins. The pale man, passing along in the shadow of the footpath, stopped in an angle. Three policemen were coming over the bridge in company—they went in threes in these parts—and the pale man, who never made closer acquaintance with the police than he could help, slunk down by the bridge-foot, as though designing to make the crossing by way of the narrow lock; no safe passage in the dark.

But he thought better of it, and went by the bridge, as soon as the policemen had passed.

A little farther and he was in Ratcliff Highway, where it joined with Shadwell High Street, and just before him stood Paddy's Goose. The house was known by that name far beyond the neighbourhood, among people who were unaware that the actual painted sign was the White Swan. Paddy's Goose was still open, for its doors never closed till one; though there were a few houses later even than this, where, though the bars were cleared and closed at one, in accordance with Act of Parliament, the doors swung wide again ten minutes later. There was still dancing within at Paddy's Goose, and the squeak of fiddles and the thump of feet were plain to hear. The pale man passed on into the dark beyond its lights, and soon the black mouth of Blue Gate stood on his right.

Blue Gate gave its part to the night's noises, and more; for a sudden burst of loud screams—a woman's—rent the air from its innermost deeps; screams which affected the pale man not at all, nor any other passenger; for it might be murder or it might be drink, or sudden rage or fear, or a quarrel; and whatever it might be was common enough in Blue Gate.

Paddy's Goose had no monopoly of music, and the common plenty of street fiddlers was the greater as the early houses closed. Scarce eighty yards from Blue Gate stood Blind George, fiddling his hardest for a party dancing in the roadway. Many were looking on, drunk or sober, with approving shouts; and every face was ghastly phosphorescent in the glare of a ship's blue-light that a noisy negro flourished among the dancers. Close by, a woman and a man were quarrelling in the middle of a group; but the matter had no attention till of a sudden it sprang into a fight, and the man and another were punching and wrestling in a heap, bare to the waist. At this the crowd turned from the dancers, and the negro ran yelping to shed his deathly light on the new scene.

The crowd howled and scrambled, and a drunken sailor fell in the mud. Quick at the chance, a ruffian took him under the armpits and dragged him from among the trampling feet to a near entry, out of the glare. There he propped his prey, with many friendly words, and dived among his pockets. The sailor was dazed, and made no difficulty; till the thief got to the end of the search in a trouser pocket, and thence pulled a handful of silver. With that the victim awoke to some sense of affairs, and made a move to rise; but the other sprang up and laid him over with a kick on the head, just as the pale man came along. The thief made off, leaving a few shillings and sixpences on the ground, which the pale man instantly gathered

26

up. He looked from the money to the man, who lay insensible, with blood about his ear; and then from the man to the money. Then he stuffed some few of the shillings into the sailor's nearest pocket and went off with the rest.

The fight rose and fell, the crowd grew, and the blue light burned down. In twenty seconds the pale man was back again. He bent over the bleeding sailor, thrust the rest of the silver into the pocket, and finally vanished into the night. For, indeed, though the pale man was poor, and though he got a living now in a way scarce reputable: yet he had once kept a chandler's shop. He had kept it till neither sand in the sugar nor holes under the weights would any longer induce it to keep him; and then he had fallen wholly from respectability. But he had drawn a line—he had always drawn a line. He had never been a thief; and, with a little struggle, he remembered it now.

Back in Blue Gate the screams had ceased. For on a black stair a large bony man shook a woman by the throat, so that she could scream no more. He cursed in whispers, and threatened her with an end of all noise if she opened her mouth again. "Ye stop out of it all this time," he said, "an' when ye come ye squall enough to bring the slops from Arbour Square!"

"O! O!" the woman gasped. "I fell on it, Dan! I fell on it! I fell on it in the dark!..."

There was nothing commoner in the black streets about the Highway than the sight of two or three men linked by the arms, staggering, singing and bawling. Many such parties went along the Highway that night, many turned up its foul tributaries; some went toward and over the bridge by the lock that was on the way to the Hole in the Wall. But they were become fewer, and the night noises of the Highway were somewhat abated, when a party of three emerged from the mouth of Blue Gate. Of them that had gone before the songs were broken and the voices unmelodious enough; yet no other song sung that night in the Highway was so wild as the song of these men—or rather of two of them, who sang the louder because of the silence of the man between them; and no other voices were so ill-governed as theirs. The man on the right was large, bony and powerful; he on the left was shorter and less to be noticed, except that under some rare and feeble lamp it might have been perceived that his face was an ugly one, with a broken nose. But what reveller so drunk, what drunkard so insensible, what clod so silent as the man they dragged between them? His feet trailed in the mire, and his head, hidden by a ragged hat, hung forward on his chest. So they went, reeling ever where the shadows were thickest,

27

toward the bridge; but in all their reelings there was a stealthy hasting forward, and an anxious outlook that went ill with their song. The song itself, void alike of tune and jollity, fell off altogether as they neared the bridge, and here they went the quicker. They turned down by the bridge foot, though not for the reason the pale man had, two hours before, for now no policeman was in sight; and soon were gone into the black shadow about the lock-head....

It was the deep of the night, and as near quiet as the Highway ever knew; with no more than a cry here or there, a distant fiddle, and the faint hum of the wind in the rigging of ships. Off in Blue Gate the woman sat on the black stair, with her face in her hands, waiting for company before returning to the room where she had fallen over something in the dark.

CHAPTER VI
STEPHEN'S TALE

High under the tiles of the Hole in the Wall, I had at first a night of disturbed sleep. I was in my old familiar cot, which had been brought during the evening, on a truck. But things were strange, and, in particular, my grandfather, who slept on the opposite side of the room, snored so amazingly, and with a sound so unlike anything I had ever heard before, that I feared he must be choking to death, and climbed out of bed, once, to see. There were noises from without too, sometimes of discordant singing, sometimes of quarrels; and once, from a distance, a succession of dreadful screams. Then the old house made curious sounds of its own; twice I was convinced of stealthy steps on the stair, and all night the very walls creaked aloud. So for long, sleepy as I was, I dozed and started and rolled and lay awake, wondering about the little ship in the bar-parlour, and Mr. Cripps, and the pale man, and the watch with the M on it. Also I considered again the matter of my prayers, which I had already discussed with Grandfather Nat, to his obvious perplexity, by candle-light. For I was urgent to know if I must now leave my mother out, and if I might not put my little dead brother in; being very anxious to include them both. My grandfather's first opinion was, that it was not the usual thing; which opinion he expressed with hesitation, and a curious look of

28

the eyes that I wondered at. But I argued that God could bless them just as well in heaven as here; and Grandfather Nat admitted that no doubt there was something in that. Whereupon I desired to know if they would hear if I said in my prayers that I was quite safe with him, at the Hole in the Wall; or if I should rather ask God to tell them. And at that my grandfather stood up and turned away, with a rub and a pat on my head, toward his own bed; telling me to say whatever I pleased, and not to forget Grandfather Nat.

So that now, having said what I pleased, and having well remembered Grandfather Nat, and slept and woke and dozed and woke again, I took solace from his authority and whispered many things to my little dead brother, whom I could never play with: of the little ship in the glass case, and the pictures, and of how I was going to the London Dock to-morrow; and so at last fell asleep soundly till morning.

Grandfather Nat was astir early, and soon I was looking from the window by his bed at the ships that lay so thick in the Pool, tier on tier. Below me I could see the water that washed between the slimy piles on which the house rested, and to the left were the narrow stairs that terminated the passage at the side. Several boats were moored about these stairs, and a waterman was already looking out for a fare. Out in the Pool certain other boats caught the eye as they dodged about among the colliers, because each carried a bright fire amidships, in a brazier, beside a man, two small barrels of beer, and a very large handbell. The men were purlmen, Grandfather Nat told me, selling liquor—hot beer chiefly, in the cold mornings—to the men on the colliers, or on any other craft thereabout. It struck me that the one thing lacking for perfect bliss in most rowing boats was just such a brazier of cosy fire as the purl-boat carried; so that after very little consideration I resolved that when I grew up I would not be a sailor, nor an engine-driver, nor any one of a dozen other things I had thought of, but a purlman.

The staircase would have landed one direct into the bar-parlour but for an enclosing door, which strangers commonly mistook for that of a cupboard. A step as light as mine was possibly a rarity on this staircase; for, coming down before my grandfather, I startled a lady in the bar-parlour who had been doing something with a bottle which involved the removal of the cork; which cork she snatched hastily from a shelf and replaced, with no very favourable regard to myself; and straightway dropped on her knees and went to work with a brush and a dustpan. She was scarce an attractive woman, I thought, being rusty and bony, slack-faced and very red-nosed. She swept the carpet and dusted the shelves with an air of angry contempt for everything she touched, and I got into the bar out of her way as soon as I could. The potman was flinging sawdust about the floor, and there, in the same corner, sat the same pale, ragged man that was there last night, with the same full glass of liquor—or one like it—by his side: like a trade fixture that had been there all night.

When Grandfather Nat appeared, I learned the slack-faced woman's name. "This here's my little gran'son, Mrs. Grimes," he said, "as is goin' to live here a bit, 'cordin' as I mentioned yesterday."

"Hindeed?" said Mrs. Grimes, with a glance that made me feel more contemptible than the humblest article she had dusted that morning. "Hindeed? Then it'll be more work more pay, Cap'en Kemp."

"Very well, mum," my grandfather replied. "If you reckon it out more work——"

"Ho!" interjected Mrs. Grimes, who could fill a misplaced aspirate with subtle offence; "reckon or not, I s'pose there's another bed to be made? An' buttons to be sewed? An' plates for to be washed? An' dirt an' litter for to be cleared up everywhere? To say nothink o' crumbs—which the biscuit-crumbs in the bar-parlour this mornin' was thick an' shameful!"

I had had biscuits, and I felt a reprobate. "Very well, mum," Grandfather Nat said, peaceably; "we'll make out extry damages, mum. A few days'll give us an idea. Shall we leave it a week an' see how things go?"

"Ham I to consider that a week's notice, Captain Kemp?" Mrs. Grimes demanded, with a distinct rise of voice. "Ham I or ham I not?"

"Notice!" My grandfather was puzzled, and began to look a trifle angry. "Why, damme, who said notice? What——"

"Because notice is as easy give as took, Cap'en Kemp, as I'd 'ave you remember. An' slave I may be though better brought up than slave-drivers any day, but swore at vulgar I won't be, nor trampled like dirt an' litter beneath the feet, an' will not endure it neither!" And with a great toss of the head Mrs. Grimes flounced through the staircase door, and sniffed and bridled her way to the upper rooms.

Her exit relieved my mind; first, because I had a wretched consciousness that I was causing all the trouble, and a dire fear that Grandfather Nat might dislike me for it; and second, because when he looked angry I had a fearful foreboding vision of Mrs. Grimes being presently whirled round by the ear and flung into the street, as Jim Crute had been. But it was not long ere I learned that Mrs.

Grimes was one of those persons who grumble and clamour and bully at everything and everybody on principle, finding that, with a concession here and another there, it pays very well on the whole; and so nag along very comfortably through life. As for herself, as I had seen, Mrs. Grimes did not lack the cunning to carry away any fit of virtuous indignation that seemed like to push her employer out of his patience.

My grandfather looked at the bottle that Mrs. Grimes had recorked.

"That rum shrub," he said, "ain't properly mixed. It works in the bottle when it's left standing, an' mounts to the cork. I notice it almost every morning."

The day was bright, and I resigned myself with some impatience to wait for an hour or two till we could set out for the docks. It was a matter of business, my grandfather explained, that he must not leave the bar till a fixed hour—ten o'clock; and soon I began to make a dim guess at the nature of the business, though I guessed in all innocence, and suspected not at all.

Contrary to my evening observation, at this early hour the larger bar was mostly empty, while the obscure compartment at the side was in far greater use than it had been last night. Four or five visitors must have come there, one after another: perhaps half a dozen. And they all had things to sell. Two had watches—one of them was a woman; one had a locket and a boatswain's silver call; and I think another had some silver spoons. Grandfather Nat brought each article into the bar-parlour, to examine, and then returned it to its owner; which behaviour seemed to surprise none of them as it had surprised the man last night; so that doubtless he was a stranger. To those with watches my grandfather said nothing but "Yes, that seems all right," or "Yes, it's a good enough watch, no doubt." But to the man with the locket and the silver call he said, "Well, if ever you want to sell 'em you might get eight bob; no more"; and much the same to him with the spoons, except that he thought the spoons might fetch fifteen shillings.

Each of the visitors went out with no more ado; and as each went, the pale man in the larger bar rose, put his drink safely on the counter, just beyond the partition, and went out too; and presently he came back, with no more than a glance at Grandfather Nat, took his drink, and sat down again.

At ten o'clock my grandfather looked out of the bar and said to the pale man: "All right—drink up."

Whereupon the pale man—who would have been paler if his face had been washed—swallowed his drink at last, flat as it must

31

have been, and went out; and Grandfather Nat went out also, by the door into the passage. He was gone scarce two minutes, and when he returned he unlocked a drawer below the shelf on which the little ship stood, and took from it the cash box I had seen last night. His back was turned toward me, and himself was interposed between my eyes and the box, which he rested on the shelf; but I heard a jingling that suggested spoons.

So I said, "Did the man go to buy the spoons for you, Gran'fa' Nat?"

My grandfather looked round sharply, with something as near a frown as he ever directed on me. Then he locked the box away hastily, with a gruff laugh. "You won't starve, Stevy," he said, "as long as wits finds victuals. But see here," he went on, becoming grave as he sat and drew me to his knee; "see here, Stevy. What you see here's my business, private business; understand? You ain't a tell-tale, are you? Not a sneak?"

I repudiated the suggestion with pain and scorn; for I was at least old enough a boy to see in sneakery the blackest of crimes.

"No, no, that you ain't, I know," Grandfather Nat went on, with a pinch of my chin, though he still regarded me earnestly. "A plucked 'un's never a sneak. But there's one thing for you to remember, Stevy, afore all your readin' an' writin' an' lessons an' what not. You must never tell of anything you see here, not to a soul—that is, not about me buyin' things. I'm very careful, but things don't always go right, an' I might get in trouble. I'm a straight man, an' I pay for all I have in any line o' trade; I never stole nor cheated not so much as a farden all my life, nor ever bought anything as I knew was stole. See?"

I nodded gravely. I was trying hard to understand the reason for all this seriousness and secrecy, but at any rate I was resolved to be no tale-bearer; especially against Grandfather Nat.

"Why," he went on, justifying himself, I fancy, more for his own satisfaction than for my information; "why, even when it's on'y just suspicious I won't buy—except o' course through another party. That's how I guard myself, Stevy, an' every man has a right to buy a thing reasonable an' sell at a profit if he can; that's on'y plain trade. An' yet nobody can't say truthful as he ever sold me anything over that there counter, or anywhere else, barrin' what I have reg'lar of the brewer an' what not. I may look at a thing or pass an opinion, but what's that? Nothin' at all. But we've got to keep our mouths shut, Stevy, for fear o' danger; see? You wouldn't like poor old Grandfather Nat to be put in gaol, would ye?"

32

The prospect was terrible, and I put my hands about my grandfather's neck and vowed I would never whisper a word.

"That's right, Stevy," the old man answered, "I know you won't if you don't forget yourself—so don't do that. Don't take no notice, not even to me."

There was a knock at the back door, which opened, and disclosed one of the purlmen, who had left his boat in sight at the stairs, and wanted a quart of gin in the large tin can he brought with him. He was a short, red-faced, tough-looking fellow, and he needed the gin, as I soon learned, to mix with his hot beer to make the purl. He had a short conversation with my grandfather when the gin was brought, of which I heard no more than the words "high water at twelve." But as he went down the passage he turned, and sang out: "You got the news, Cap'en, o' course?"

"What? Viney and Marr?"

The man nodded, with a click and a twitch of the mouth. Then he snapped his fingers, and jerked them expressively upward. After which he ejaculated the single word "Marr," and jerked his thumb over his shoulder. By which I understood him to repeat, with no waste of language, the story that it was all up with the firm, and the junior partner had bolted.

"That," said Grandfather Nat, when the man was gone—"that's Bill Stagg, an' he's the on'y purlman as don't come ashore to sleep. Sleeps in his boat, winter an' summer, does Bill Stagg. How'd you like that, Stevy?"

I thought I should catch cold, and perhaps tumble overboard, if I had a bad dream; and I said so.

"Ah well, Bill Stagg don't mind. He was A.B. aboard o' me when Mr. Viney was my mate many years ago, an' a good A.B. too. Bill Stagg, he makes fast somewhere quiet at night, an' curls up snug as a weevil. Mostly under the piles o' this here house, when the wind ain't east. Saves him rent, ye see; so he does pretty well."

And with that my grandfather put on his coat and reached the pilot cap that was his everyday wear.

CHAPTER VII
STEPHEN'S TALE

We walked first to the head of the stairs, where opened a wide picture of the Thames and all its traffic, and where the walls were plastered with a dozen little bills, each headed "Found Drowned," and each with the tale of some nameless corpse under the heading.

"That's my boat, Stevy," said my grandfather, pointing to a little dinghy with a pair of sculls in her; "our boat, if you like, seeing as we're pardners. Now you shall do which you like; walk along to the dock, where the sugar is, or come out in our boat."

It was a hard choice to make. The glory and delight of the part ownership of a real boat dazzled me like another sun in the sky; but I had promised myself the docks and the sugar for such a long time. So we compromised; the docks to-day and the boat to-morrow.

Out in the street everybody seemed to know Grandfather Nat. Those who spoke with him commonly called him Captain Kemp, except a few old acquaintances to whom he was Captain Nat. Loafers and crimps gazed after him and nodded together; and small ship-chandlers gave him good morning from their shop-doors.

A hundred yards from the Hole in the Wall, at a turn, there was a swing bridge and a lock, such as we had by the old house in Blackwall. At the moment we came in hail the men were at the winch, and the bridge began to part in the middle; for a ship was about to change berth to the inner dock. "Come, Stevy," said my grandfather, "we'll take the lock 'fore they open that. Not afraid if I'm with you, are you?"

No, I was not afraid with Grandfather Nat, and would not even be carried. Though the top of the lock was not two feet wide, and was knotted, broken and treacherous in surface and wholly unguarded on one side, where one looked plump down into the foul dock-water; and though on the other side there was but a slack chain strung through loose iron stanchions that staggered in their sockets. Grandfather Nat gripped me by the collar and walked me before him; but relief tempered my triumph when I was safe across; my feet never seemed to have twisted and slipped and stumbled so much before in so short a distance—perhaps because in that same distance I had never before recollected so many tales of men drowned in the docks by falling off just such locks, in fog, or by accidental slips.

A little farther along, and we came upon Ratcliff Highway. I saw the street then for the first time, and in truth it was very wonderful. I think there could never have been another street in this country at once so foul and so picturesque as Ratcliff Highway at the time I speak of. Much that I saw I could not understand, child as I was; and by so much the more was I pleased with it all, when perhaps I should have been shocked. From end to end of the

Highway and beyond, and through all its tributaries and purlieus everything and everybody was for, by, and of, the sailor ashore; every house and shop was devoted to his convenience and inconvenience; in the Highway it seemed to me that every other house was a tavern, and in several places two stood together. There were shops full of slops, sou'westers, pilot-coats, sea-boots, tin pannikins, and canvas kit-bags like giants' bolsters; and rows of big knives and daggers, often engraved with suggestive maxims. A flash of memory recalls the favourite: "Never draw me without cause, never sheathe me without honour." I have since seen the words "cause" and "honour" put to uses less respectable.

The pawn-shops had nothing in them that had not come straight from a ship—sextants and boatswain's pipes being the choice of the stock. And pawn-shops, slop-shops, tobacco-shops—every shop almost—had somewhere in its window a selection of those curiosities that sailors make abroad and bring home: little ship-models mysteriously erected inside bottles, shells, albatross heads, saw-fish snouts, and bottles full of sand of different colours, ingeniously packed so as to present a figure or a picture when viewed from without.

Men of a dozen nations were coming or going in every score of yards. The best dressed, and the worst, were the negroes; for the black cook who was flush went in for adornments that no other sailor-man would have dreamed of: a white shirt, a flaming tie, a black coat with satin facings—even a white waistcoat and a top hat. While the cleaned-out and shipless nigger was a sad spectacle indeed. Then there were Spaniards, swart, long-haired, bloodshot-looking fellows, whose entire shore outfit consisted commonly of a red shirt, blue trousers, anklejacks with the brown feet visible over them, a belt, a big knife, and a pair of large gold ear-rings. Big, yellow-haired, blue-eyed Swedes, who were full pink with sea and sun, and not brown or mahogany-coloured, like the rest; slight, wicked-looking Malays; lean, spitting Yankees, with stripes, and felt hats, and sing-song oaths; sometimes a Chinaman, petticoated, dignified, jeered at; a Lascar, a Greek, a Russian; and everywhere the English Jack, rolling of gait—sometimes from habit alone, sometimes for mixed reasons—hard, red-necked, waistcoatless, with his knife at his belt, like the rest: but more commonly a clasp-knife than one in a sheath. To me all these strangely bedight men were matter of delight and wonder; and I guessed my hardest whence each had come last, what he had brought in his ship, and what strange and desperate adventures he had encountered on the way. And wherever I saw bare, hairy skin, whether an arm, or the chest under an open shirt, there were blue devices of ships, of flags, of women, of letters and names. Grandfather Nat was tattooed like that, as I had discovered in the morning, when he washed. He had been a fool to have it done, he said, as he flung the soapy water out of window into the river, and he warned me that I must be careful never to make such a mistake myself; which made me sorry, because it seemed so gallant an embellishment. But my grandfather explained that you could be identified by tattoo-marks, at any length of time, which might cause trouble. I remembered that my own father was tattooed with an anchor and my mother's name; and I hoped he would never be identified, if it were as bad as that.

In the street oyster-stalls stood, and baked-potato cans; one or two sailors were buying, and one or two fiddlers, but mostly the customers were the gaudy women, who seemed to make a late breakfast in this way. Some had not stayed to perform a greater toilet than to fling clothes on themselves unhooked and awry, and to make a straggling knot of their hair; but the most were brilliant enough in violet or scarlet or blue, with hair oiled and crimped and hung in thick nets, and with bright handkerchiefs over their shoulders—belcher yellows and kingsmen and blue billies. And presently we came on one who was dancing with a sailor on the pavement, to the music of one of the many fiddlers who picked up a living hereabouts; and she wore the regular dancing rig of the Highway—short skirts and high red morocco boots with brass heels. She covered the buckle and grape-vined with great precision, too, a contrast with her partner, whose hornpipe was unsteady and vague in the figures, for indeed he seemed to have "begun early"—perhaps had not left off all night. Two more pairs of these red morocco boots we saw at a place next a public house, where a shop front had been cleared out to make a dancing room, with a sort of buttery-hatch communicating with the tavern; and where a flushed sailor now stood with a pot in each hand, roaring for a fiddler.

But if the life and the picturesqueness of the Highway in some sort disguised its squalor, they made the more hideously apparent the abomination of the by-streets: which opened, filthy and menacing, at every fifty yards as we went. The light seemed greyer, the very air thicker and fouler in these passages; though indeed they formed the residential part whereof the Highway was the market-place. The children who ran and tumbled in these places, the boy of nine equally with the infant crawling from doorstep to gutter, were half naked, shoeless, and disguised in crusted foulness; so that I remember them with a certain sickening, even in these latter days;

when I see no such pitiably neglected little wretches, though I know the dark parts of London well enough.

At the mouth of one of these narrow streets, almost at the beginning of the Highway, Grandfather Nat stopped and pointed.

It was a forbidding lane, with forbidding men and women hanging about the entrance; and far up toward the end there appeared to be a crowd and a fight; in the midst whereof a half-naked man seemed to be rushing from side to side of the street.

"That's the Blue Gate," said my grandfather, and resumed his walk. "It's dangerous," he went on, "the worst place hereabout—perhaps anywhere. Wuss'n Tiger Bay, a mile. You must never go near Blue Gate. People get murdered there, Stevy—murdered—many's a man; sailor-men mostly; an' nobody never knows. Pitch them in the Dock sometimes, sometimes in the river, so's they're washed away. I've known 'em taken to Hole-in-the-Wall Stairs at night."

I gripped my grandfather's hand tighter, and asked, in all innocence, if we should see any, if we kept watch out of window that night. He laughed, thought the chance scarce worth a sleepless night, and went on to tell me of something else. But I overheard later in a bar conversation a ghastly tale of years before; of a murdered man's body that had been dragged dripping through the streets at night by two men who supported its arms, staggering and shouting and singing, as though the three were merely drunk; and how it was dropped in panic ere it was brought to the waterside, because of a collision with three live sailors who really were drunk.

One or two crimps' carts came through from the docks as we walked, drawn by sorry animals, and piled high with shouting sailors and their belongings—chief among these the giant bolster-bags. The victims went to their fate gloriously enough, hailing and chaffing the populace on the way, and singing, each man as he list. Also we saw a shop with a window full of parrots and monkeys; and a very sick kangaroo in a wooden cage being carried in from a van.

And so we came to the London Dock at last. And there, in the sugar-sheds, stood more sugar than ever I had dreamed of in my wildest visions—thousands of barrels, mountains of sacks. And so many of the bags were rat-bitten, or had got a slit by accidentally running up against a jack-knife; and so many of the barrels were defective, or had stove themselves by perverse complications with a crowbar; that the heavy, brown, moist stuff was lying in heaps and lumps everywhere; and I supposed that it must be called "foot-sugar" because you couldn't help treading on it.

It was while I was absorbed in this delectable spectacle, that I

37

heard a strained little voice behind me, and turned to behold Mr. Cripps greeting my grandfather.

"Good mornin', Cap'en Kemp, sir," said Mr. Cripps. "I been a-lookin' at the noo Blue Crosser—the Emily Riggs. She ought to be done, ye know, an' a han'some picter she'd make; but the skipper seems busy. Why, an' there's young master Stephen, I do declare; 'ow are ye, sir?"

As he bent and the nose neared, I was seized with a horrid fear that he was going to kiss me. But he only shook hands, after all—though it was not at all a clean hand that he gave.

"Why, Cap'en Kemp," he went on, "this is what I say a phenomenal coincidence; rather unique, in fact. Why, you'll 'ardly believe as I was a thinkin' o' you not 'arf an hour ago, scarcely! Now you wouldn't 'a' thought that, would ye?"

There was a twinkle in Grandfather Nat's eye. "All depends," he said.

"Comin' along from the mortuary, I see somethink——"

"Ah, something in the mortuary, no doubt," my grandfather interrupted, quizzically. "Well, what was in the mortuary? I bet there was a corpse in the mortuary."

"Quite correct, Cap'en Kemp, so there was; three of 'em, an' a very sad sight; decimated, Cap'en Kemp, by the watery element. But it wasn't them I was——"

"What! It wasn't a corpse as reminded you of me? That's rum. Then I expect somebody told you some more about Viney and Marr. Come, what's the latest about Viney an' Marr? Tell us about that."

Grandfather Nat was humorously bent on driving Mr. Cripps from his mark, and Mr. Cripps deferred. "Well, it's certainly a topic," he said, "a universal topic. Crooks the ship-chandler's done for, they say—unsolvent. The Minerva's reported off Prawle Point in to-day's list, an' they say as she'll be sold up as soon as she's moored. But there—she's hypotenused, Cap'en Kemp; pawned, as you might say; up the flue. It's a matter o' gen'ral information that she's pawned up to 'er r'yals—up to 'er main r'yals, sir. Which reminds me, speakin' o' r'yals, there's a timber-shop just along by the mortuary——"

"Ah, no doubt," Grandfather Nat interrupted, "they must put 'em somewhere. Any news o' the Juno?"

"No, sir, she ain't reported; not doo Barbadoes yet, or mail not in, any'ow. They'll sell 'er too, but the creditors won't get none of it. She's hypotenused as deep as the other—up to her r'yals; an' there's nothin' else to sell. So it's the gen'ral opinion there won't be much to

38

divide, Marr 'avin' absconded with the proceeds. An' as regards what I was agoin' to——"

"Yes, you was goin' to tell me some more about Marr, I expect," my grandfather persisted. "Heard where he's gone?"

Mr. Cripps shook his head. "They don't seem likely to ketch 'im, Cap'en Nat. Some says 'e's absconded out o' the country, others says 'e's 'idin' in it. Nobody knows 'im much, consequence o' Viney doin' all the outdoor business—I on'y see 'im once myself. Viney, 'e thinks 'e's gone abroad, they say; an' 'e swears Marr's the party as 'as caused the unsolvency, 'avin' bin a-doin' of 'im all along; 'im bein' in charge o' the books. An' it's a fact, Cap'en Kemp, as you never know what them chaps may get up to with the proceeds as 'as charge o' books. The paper's full of 'em every week—always absconding with somebody's proceeds! An' by the way, speakin' o' proceeds——"

This time Captain Nat made no interruption, but listened with an amused resignation.

"Speakin' o' proceeds," said Mr. Cripps, "it was bein' temp'ry out o' proceeds as made me think o' you as I come along from the mortuary. For I see as 'andsome a bit o' panel for to paint a sign on as ever I come across. It was——"

"Yes, I know. Enough to stimilate you to paint it fine, only to look at it, wasn't it?"

"Well, yes, Cap'n Kemp, so it was."

"Not dear, neither?"

"No—not to say dear, seein' 'ow prices is up. If I'd 'ad——"

"Well, well, p'raps prices'll be down a bit soon," said Grandfather Nat, grinning and pulling out a sixpence. "I ain't good for no more than that now, anyhow!" And having passed over the coin he took my hand and turned away, laughing and shaking his head.

Seeing that my grandfather wanted his sign, it seemed to me that he was losing an opportunity, and I said so.

"What!" he said, "let him buy the board? Why, he's had half a dozen boards for that sign a'ready!"

"Half a dozen?" I said. "Six boards? What did he do with them?"

"Ate 'em!" said Grandfather Nat, and laughed the louder when I stared.

CHAPTER VIII
STEPHEN'S TALE

I found it quite true that one might eat the loose sugar wherever he judged it clean enough—as most of it was. And nothing but Grandfather Nat's restraining hand postponed my first bilious attack.

Thus it was that I made acquaintance with the Highway, and with the London Docks, in their more picturesque days, and saw and delighted in a thousand things more than I can write. Port was drunk then, and hundreds of great pipes lay in rows on a wide quay where men walked with wooden clubs, whacking each pipe till the "shive" or wooden bung sprang into the air, to be caught with a dexterity that pleased me like a conjuring trick. And many a thirsty dock-labourer, watching his opportunity, would cut a strip of bread from his humble dinner as he strolled near a pipe, and, absorbed in the contemplation of the indefinite empyrean, absently dip his sippet into the shive-hole as he passed; recovering it in a state so wet and discoloured that its instant consumption was imperative.

And so at last we came away from the docks by the thoroughfare then called Tanglefoot Lane; not that that name, or anything like it, was painted at the corner; but because it was the road commonly taken by visitors departing from the wine-vaults after bringing tasting-orders.

As we passed Blue Gate on our way home, I saw, among those standing at the corner, a coarse-faced, untidy woman, talking to a big, bony-looking man with a face so thin and mean that it seemed misplaced on such shoulders. The woman was so much like a score of others then in sight, that I should scarce have noted her, were it not that she and the man stopped their talk as we passed, with a quick look, first at my grandfather, and then one at the other; and then the man turned his back and walked away. Presently the woman came after us, walking quickly, glancing doubtfully at Grandfather Nat as she passed; and at last, after twice looking back, she turned and waited for us to come up.

"Beg pardon, Cap'en Kemp," she said in a low, but a very thick voice, "but might I speak to you a moment, sir?"

My grandfather looked at her sharply. "Well," he said, "what is it?"

"In regards to a man as sold you a watch las' night——"

40

"No," Grandfather Nat interrupted with angry decision, "he didn't."

"Beg pardon, sir, jesso sir—'course not; which I mean to say 'e sold it to a man near to your 'ouse. Is it brought true as that party—not meanin' you, sir, 'course not, but the party in the street near your 'ouse—is it brought true as that party'll buy somethink more—somethink as I needn't tell now, sir, p'raps, but somethink spoke of between that party an' the other party—I mean the party as sold it, an' don't mean you, sir, 'course not?"

It was plain that the woman, who had begun in trepidation, was confused and abashed the more by the hard frown with which Captain Nat regarded her. The frown persisted for some moments; and then my grandfather said: "Don't know what you mean. If somebody bought anything of a friend o' yours, an' your friend wants to sell him something else, I suppose he can take it to him, can't he? And if it's any value, there's no reason he shouldn't buy it, so far as I know." And Grandfather Nat strode on.

The woman murmured some sort of acknowledgment, and fell back, and in a moment I had forgotten her; though I remembered her afterward, for good reason enough.

In fact, it was no later than that evening. I was sitting in the bar-parlour with Grandfather Nat, who had left the bar to the care of the potman. My grandfather was smoking his pipe, while I spelled and sought down the narrow columns of Lloyd's List for news of my father's ship. It was my grandfather's way to excuse himself from reading, when he could, on the plea of unsuitable eyes; though I suspect that, apart from his sight, he found reading a greater trouble than he was pleased to own.

"There's nothing here about the Juno, Grandfather Nat," I said. "Nothing anywhere."

"Ah," said my grandfather, "La Guaira was the last port, an' we must keep eyes on the list for Barbadoes. Maybe the mail's late." Most of Lloyd's messages came by mail at that time. "Let's see," he went on; "Belize, La Guaira, Barbadoes"; and straightway began to figure out distances and chances of wind.

Grandfather Nat had been considering whether or not we should write to my father to tell him that my mother was dead, and he judged that there was little chance of any letter reaching the Juno on her homeward passage.

"Belize, La Guaira, Barbadoes," said Grandfather Nat, musingly. "It's the rough reason thereabout, an' it's odds she may be blown out of her course. But the mail——"

He stopped and turned his head. There was a sudden stamp of

41

feet outside the door behind us, a low and quick voice, a heavy thud against the door, and then a cry—a dreadful cry, that began like a stifled scream and ended with a gurgle.

Grandfather Nat reached the door at a bound, and as he flung it wide a man came with it and sank heavily at his feet, head and one shoulder over the threshold, and an arm flung out stiffly, so that the old man stumbled across it as he dashed at a dark shadow without.

I was hard at my grandfather's heels, and in a flash of time I saw that another man was rising from over the one on the doorsill. But for the stumble Grandfather Nat would have had him. In that moment's check the fellow spun round and dashed off, striking one of the great posts with his shoulder, and nearly going down with the shock.

All was dark without, and what I saw was merely confused by the light from the bar-parlour. My grandfather raised a shout and rushed in the wake of the fugitive, toward the stairs, and I, too startled and too excited to be frightened yet, skipped over the stiff arm to follow him. At the first step I trod on some object which I took to be my grandfather's tobacco-pouch, snatched it up, and stuffed it in my jacket pocket as I ran. Several men from the bar were running in the passage, and down the stairs I could hear Captain Nat hallooing across the river.

"Ahoy!" came a voice in reply. "What's up?" And I could see the fire of a purl-boat coming in.

"Stop him, Bill!" my grandfather shouted. "Stop him! Stabbed a man! He's got my boat, and there's no sculls in this damned thing! Gone round them barges!"

And now I could distinguish my grandfather in a boat, paddling desperately with a stretcher, his face and his shirt-sleeves touched with the light from the purl-man's fire.

The purl-boat swung round and shot off, and presently other boats came pulling by, with shouts and questions. Then I saw Grandfather Nat, a black form merely, climbing on a barge and running and skipping along the tier, from one barge to another, calling and directing, till I could see him no more. There were many men on the stairs by this time, and others came running and jostling; so I made my way back to the bar-parlour door.

It was no easy thing to get in here, for a crowd was gathering. But a man from the bar who recognised me made a way, and as soon as I had pushed through the crowd of men's legs I saw that the injured man was lying on the floor, tended by the potman; while Mr. Cripps, his face pallid under the dirt, and his nose a deadly lavender, stood by, with his mouth open and his hands dangling aimlessly.

The stabbed man lay with his head on a rolled-up coat of my grandfather's, and he was bad for a child to look at. His face had gone tallowy; his eyes, which turned (and frightened me) as I came in, were now directed steadily upward; he breathed low and quick, and though Joe the potman pressed cloths to the wound in his chest, there was blood about his lips and chin, and blood bubbled dreadfully in his mouth. But what startled me most, and what fixed my regard on his face despite my tremors, so that I could scarce take my eyes from it, was the fact that, paleness and blood and drawn cheeks notwithstanding, I saw in him the ugly, broken-nosed fellow who had been in the private compartment last night, with a watch to sell; the watch, with an initial on the back, that now lay in Grandfather Nat's cash-box.

CHAPTER IX
STEPHEN'S TALE

Somebody had gone for a doctor, it was said, but a doctor was not always easy to find in Wapping. Mrs. Grimes, who was at some late work upstairs, was not disturbed at first by the noise, since excitement was not uncommon in the neighbourhood. But now she came to the stairfoot door, and peeped and hurried back. For myself, I squeezed into a far corner and stared, a little sick; for there was a deal of blood, and Joe the potman was all dabbled, like a slaughterman.

My grandfather returned almost on the doctor's heels, and with my grandfather were some river police, in glazed hats and pilot coats. The doctor puffed and shook his head, called for cold water, and cloths, and turpentine, and milk. Cold water and cloths were ready enough, and turpentine was easy to get, but ere the milk came it was useless. The doctor shook his head and puffed more than ever, wiped his hands and pulled his cuffs down gingerly. I could not see the man on the floor, now, for the doctor was in the way; but I heard him, just before the doctor stood up. The noise sent my neck cold at the back; though indeed it was scarce more than the noise made in emptying a large bottle by up-ending it.

43

The doctor stood up and shook his head. "Gone," he said. "And I couldn't have done more than keep him alive a few minutes, at best. It was the lung, and bad—two places. Have they got the man?"

"No," said Grandfather Nat, "nor ain't very likely, I'd say. Never saw him again, once he got behind a tier o' lighters. Waterside chap, certain; knows the river well enough, an' these stairs. I couldn't ha' got that boat o' mine off quicker, not myself."

"Ah," said one of the river policemen, "he's a waterside chap, that's plain enough. Any other 'ud a-bolted up the street. Never said nothing, did he—this one?" He was bending over the dead man; while the others cleared the people back from the door, and squeezed Mr. Cripps out among them.

"No, not a word," answered Joe the potman. "Couldn't. Tried to nod once when I spoke to 'im, but it seemed to make 'im bleed faster."

"Know him, Cap'en Nat?" asked the sergeant.

"No," answered my grandfather, "I don't know him. Might ha' seen him hanging about p'raps. But then I see a lot doin' that."

I wondered if Grandfather Nat had already forgotten about the silver watch with the M on it, or if he had merely failed to recognise the man. But I remembered what he had said in the morning, after he had bought the spoons, and I reflected that I had best hold my tongue.

And now voices without made it known that the shore police were here, with a stretcher; and presently, with a crowding and squeezing in the little bar-parlour that drove me deeper into my corner and farther under the shelf, the uncomely figure was got from the floor to the stretcher, and so out of the house.

It was plain that my grandfather was held in good regard by the police; and I think that his hint that a drop of brandy was at the service of anybody who felt the job unpleasant might have been acted on, if there had not been quite as many present at once. When at last they were gone, and the room clear, he kicked into a heap the strip of carpet that the dead man had lain on; and as he did it, he perceived me in my corner.

"What—you here all the time, Stevy?" he said. "I thought you'd gone upstairs. Here—it ain't right for boys in general, but you've got a turn; drink up this."

I believe I must have been pale, and indeed I felt a little sick now that the excitement was over. The thing had been very near, and the blood tainted the very air. So that I gulped the weak brandy and water without much difficulty, and felt better. Out in the bar Mr. Cripps's thin voice was raised in thrilling description.

Feeling better, as I have said, and no longer faced with the melancholy alternatives of crying or being ill, I bethought me of my grandfather's tobacco-pouch. "You dropped your pouch, Gran'father Nat," I said, "and I picked it up when I ran out."

And with that I pulled out of my jacket pocket—not the pouch at all; but a stout buckled pocket-book of about the same size.

"That ain't a pouch, Stevy," said Grandfather Nat; "an' mine's here in my pocket. Show me."

He opened the flap, and stood for a moment staring. Then he looked up hastily, turned his back to the bar, and sat down. "Whew! Stevy!" he said, with amazement in his eyes and the pocket-book open in his hand; "you're in luck; luck, my boy. See!"

Once more he glanced quickly over his shoulder, toward the bar; and then took in his fingers a folded bunch of paper, and opened it. "Notes!" he said, in a low voice, drawing me to his side. "Bank of England notes, every one of 'em! Fifties, an' twenties, an' tens, an' fives! Where was it?"

I told him how I had run out at his heels, had trodden on the thing in the dark, and had slipped it into my pocket, supposing it to be his old leather tobacco-pouch, from which he had but just refilled his pipe; and how I had forgotten about it, in my excitement, till the people were gone, and the brandy had quelled my faintness.

"Well, well," commented Grandfather Nat, "it's a wonderful bit o' luck, anyhow. This is what the chap was pulling away from him when I opened the door, you can lay to that; an' he lost it when he hit the post, I'll wager; unless the other pitched it away. But that's neither here nor there.... What's that?" He turned his head quickly. "That stairfoot door ain't latched again, Stevy. Made me jump: fancied it was the other."

There was nothing else in the pocket-book, it would seem, except an old photograph. It was a faded, yellowish thing, and it represented a rather stout woman, seated, with a boy of about fourteen at her side; both very respectably dressed in the fashion of twenty years earlier. Grandfather Nat put it back, and slipped the pocket-book into the same cash-box that had held the watch with the M engraved on its back.

The stairfoot door clicked again, and my grandfather sent me to shut it. As I did so I almost fancied I could hear soft footsteps ascending. But then I concluded I was mistaken; for in a few moments Mrs. Grimes was plainly heard coming downstairs, with an uncommonly full tread; and presently she presented herself.

"Good law, Cap'en Kemp," exclaimed Mrs. Grimes, with a hand clutching at her chest, and her breath a tumultuous sigh; "Good law! I am that bad! What with extry work, an' keepin' on late, an' murders under my very nose, I cannot a-bear it—no!" And she sank into a chair by the stairfoot door, letting go her brush and dustpan with a clatter.

Grandfather Nat turned to get the brandy-bottle again. Mrs. Grimes's head drooped faintly, and her eyelids nearly closed. Nevertheless I observed that the eyes under the lids were very sharp indeed, following my grandfather's back, and traversing the shelf where he had left the photograph; yet when he brought the brandy, he had to rouse her by a shake.

CHAPTER X
STEPHEN'S TALE

I went to bed early that night—as soon as Mrs. Grimes was gone, in fact. My grandfather had resolved that such a late upsitting as last night's must be no more than an indulgence once in a way. He came up with me, bringing the cash-box to put away in the little wall-cupboard against his bed-head where it always lay, at night, with a pistol by its side. Grandfather Nat peeped to see the pocket-book safe once more, and chuckled as he locked it away. This done, he sat by my side, and talked till I began to fall asleep.

The talk was of the pocket-book, and what should be done with the money. Eight hundred pounds was the sum, and two five-pound notes over, and I wondered why a man with so much money should come, the evening before, to sell his watch.

"Looks as though the money wasn't his, don't it?" commented Grandfather Nat. "Though anyhow it's no good to him now. You found it, an' it's yours, Stevy."

I remembered certain lessons of my mother's as to one's proper behaviour toward lost property, and I mentioned them. But Grandfather Nat clearly resolved me that this was no case in point. "It can't be his, because he's dead," Captain Nat argued; "an' if it's the other chap's—well, let him come an' ask for it. That's fair enough, you know, Stevy. An' if he don't come—it ain't likely he will, is it?—then it's yours; and I'll keep it to help start you in life when you grow up. I won't pay it into the bank—not for a bit, anyhow. There's numbers on bank notes: an' they lead to trouble, often. But they're as good one time as another, an' easy sent abroad later on, or what not. So there you are, my boy! Eight hundred odd to start you like a gentleman, with as much more as Grandfather Nat can put to it. Eh?"

He kissed me and rubbed his hands in my curls, and I took the occasion to communicate my decision as to being a purlman. Grandfather Nat laughed, and patted my head down on the pillow; and for a little I remembered no more.

I awoke in an agony of nightmare. The dead man, with blood streaming from mouth and eyes, was dragging my grandfather down into the river, and my mother with my little dead brother in her arms called me to throw out the pocket-book, and save him; and throw I could not, for the thing seemed glued to my fingers. So I awoke with a choke and a cry, and sat up in bed.

All was quiet about me, and below were the common evening noises of the tavern; laughs, argumentation, and the gurgle of drawn beer; though there was less noise now than when I had come up, and I judged it not far from closing time. Out in the street a woman was singing a ballad; and I got out of bed and went to the front room window to see and to hear; for indeed I was out of sorts and nervous, and wished to look at people.

At the corner of the passage there was a small group who pointed and talked together—plainly discussing the murder; and as one or two drifted away, so one or two more came up to join those remaining. No doubt the singing woman had taken this pitch as one suitable to her ware—for she sang and fluttered at length in her hand one of the versified last dying confessions that even so late as this were hawked about Ratcliff and Wapping. What murderer's "confession" the woman was singing I have clean forgotten; but they were all the same, all set to a doleful tune which, with modifications, still does duty, I believe, as an evening hymn; and the burden ran thus, for every murderer and any murder:—

Take warning by my dreadful fate, The truth I can't deny; This dreadful crime that I are done I are condemned to die.

The singular grammar of the last two lines I never quite understood, not having noticed its like elsewhere; but I put it down as a distinguishing characteristic of the speech of murderers.

I waited till the woman had taken her ballads away, and I had grown uncommonly cold in the legs, and then crept back to bed. But now I had fully awakened myself, and sleep was impossible. Presently I got up again, and looked out over the river. Very black

47

and mysterious it lay, the blacker, it seemed, for the thousand lights that spotted it, craft and shore. No purlmen's fires were to be seen, for work on the colliers was done long ago, but once a shout and now a hail came over the water, faint or loud, far or near; and up the wooden wall I leaned on came the steady sound of the lapping against the piles below. I wondered where Grandfather Nat's boat—our boat—lay now; if the murderer were still rowing in it, and would row and row right away to sea, where my father was, in his ship; or if he would be caught, and make a dying confession with all the "haves" and "ams" replaced by "ares"; or if, indeed, he had already met providential retribution by drowning. In which case I doubted for the safety of the boat, and Grandfather would buy another. And my legs growing cold again, I retreated once more.

I heard the customers being turned into the street, and the shutters going up; and then I got under the bed-clothes, for I recalled the nightmare, and it was not pleasant. It grew rather worse, indeed, for my waking fancy enlarged and embellished it, and I longed to hear the tread of Grandfather Nat ascending the stair. But he was late to-night. I heard Joe the potman, who slept off the premises, shut the door and go off up the street. For a few minutes Grandfather Nat was moving about the bar and the bar-parlour; and then there was silence, save for the noises—the clicks and the creaks—that the old house made of itself.

I waited and waited, sometimes with my head out of the clothes, sometimes with no more than a contrived hole next my ear, listening. Till at last I could wait no longer, for the house seemed alive with stealthy movement, and I shook with the indefinite terror that comes, some night or another, to the most unimaginative child. I thought, at first, of calling to my grandfather, but that would seem babyish; so I said my prayers over again, held my breath, and faced the terrors of the staircase. The boards sang and creaked under my bare feet, and the black about me was full of dim coloured faces. But I pushed the door and drew breath in the honest lamplight of the bar-parlour at last.

Nobody was there, and nobody was in the bar. Could he have gone out? Was I alone in the house, there, where the blood was still on the carpet? But there was a slight noise from behind the stairs, and I turned to look farther.

Behind the bar-parlour and the staircase were two rooms, that projected immediately over the river, with their frames resting on the piles. One was sometimes used as a parlour for the reception of mates and skippers, though such customers were rare; the other held cases, bottles and barrels. To this latter I turned, and mounting the three steps behind the staircase, pushed open the door; and was mightily astonished at what I saw.

There was my grandfather, kneeling, and there was one half of Bill Stagg the purlman, standing waist-deep in the floor. For a moment it was beyond me to guess what he was standing on, seeing that there was nothing below but water; but presently I reasoned that the tide was high, and he must be standing in his boat. He was handing my grandfather some small packages, and he saw me at once and pointed. Grandfather Nat turned sharply, and stared, and for a moment I feared he was angry. Then he grinned, shook his finger at me, and brought it back to his lips with a tap.

"All right—my pardner," he whispered, and Bill Stagg grinned too. The business was short enough, and in a few seconds Bill Stagg, with another grin at me, and something like a wink, ducked below. My grandfather, with noiseless care, put back in place a trap-door—not a square, noticeable thing, but a clump of boards of divers lengths that fell into place with as innocent an aspect as the rest of the floor. This done, he rolled a barrel over the place, and dropped the contents of the packages into a row of buckets that stood near.

"What's that, Grandfather Nat?" I ventured to ask, when all was safely accomplished.

My grandfather grinned once more, and shook his head. "Go on," he said, "I'll tell you in the bar-parlour. May as well now as let ye find out." He blew out the light of his candle and followed me.

"Well," he said, wrapping my cold feet in my nightgown as I sat on his knee. "What brought ye down, Stevy? Did we make a noise?"

I shook my head. "I—I felt lonely," I said.

"Lonely? Well, never mind. An' so ye came to look for me, eh? Well, now, this is another one o' the things as you mustn't talk about, Stevy—a little secret between ourselves, bein' pardners."

"The stuff in the pail, Gran'fa' Nat?"

"The stuff in the pail, an' the hole in the floor. You're sure you won't get talkin', an' get your poor old gran'father in trouble?"

Yes, I was quite sure; though I could not see as yet what there was to cause trouble.

"The stuff Bill Stagg brought, Stevy, is 'bacca. 'Bacca smashed down so hard that a pound ain't bigger than that matchbox. An' I pitch it in the water to swell it out again; see?"

I still failed to understand the method of its arrival. "Did Bill Stagg steal it, gran'father?" I asked.

Grandfather Nat laughed. "No, my boy," he said; "he bought it, an' I buy it. It comes off the Dutch boats. But it comes a deal

49

cheaper takin' it in that way at night-time. There's a big place I'll show you one day, Stevy—big white house just this side o' London Bridge. There's a lot o' gentlemen there as wants to see all the 'bacca that comes in from aboard, an' they take a lot o' trouble over it, and charge too, fearful. So they're very angry if parties—same as you an' me—takes any in without lettin' 'em know, an' payin' 'em the money. An' they can get you locked up."

This seemed a very unjust world that I had come into, in which Grandfather Nat was in danger of such terrible penalties for such innocent transactions—buying a watch, or getting his tobacco cheap. So I said: "I think people are very wicked in this place."

"Ah!" said my grandfather, "I s'pose none of us ain't over good. But there—I've told you about it now, an' that's better than lettin' you wonder, an' p'raps go asking other people questions. So now you know, Stevy. We've got our little secrets between us, an' you've got to keep 'em between us, else—well, you know. Nothing about anything I buy, nor about what I take in there,"—with a jerk of the thumb—"nor about 'bacca in buckets o' water."

"Nor about the pocket-book, Gran'fa' Nat?"

"Lord no. 'Specially not about that. You see, Stevy, pardners is pardners, an' they must stick together, eh? We'll stick together, won't we?"

I nodded hard and reached for my grandfather's neck.

"Ah, that we will. What others like to think they can; they can't prove nothing, nor it wouldn't be their game. But we're pardners, an' I've told you what—well, what you might ha' found out in a more awkward way. An' it ain't so bad a thing to have a pardner to talk to, neither. I never had one till now—not since your gran'mother died, that you never saw, Stevy; an' that was twenty years ago. I been alone most o' my life—not even a boy, same as it might be you. 'Cause why? When your father was your age, an' older, I was always at sea, an' never saw him, scarcely; same as him an' you now."

And indeed Grandfather Nat and I knew each other better than my father knew either of us. And so we sat for a few minutes talking of ourselves, and once more of the notes in the pocket-book upstairs; till the tramp of the three policemen on the beat stayed in the street without, and we heard one of the three coming down the passage.

He knocked sharply at the bar-parlour door, and Grandfather Nat put me down and opened it.

"Good evenin', Cap'en Kemp," said the policeman. "We knew

you was up, seein' a bit o' light." Then he leaned farther in, and in a lower voice, said: "He ain't been exactly identified yet, but it's thought some of our chaps knows 'im. Know if anything's been picked up?"

My heart gave a jump, as probably did my grandfather's. "Picked up?" he repeated. "Why, what? What d'ye mean?"

"Well, there was nothing partic'lar on the body, an' our chaps didn't see the knife. We thought if anybody about 'ad picked up anything, knife or what not, you might 'ear. So there ain't nothing?"

"No," Grandfather Nat answered blankly. "I've seen no knife, nor heard of none."

"All right, Cap'en Kemp—if you do hear of anything, give us the tip. Good night!"

Grandfather Nat looked oddly at me, and I at him. I think we had a feeling that our partnership was sealed. And so with no more words we went to bed.

CHAPTER XI
STEPHEN'S TALE

I had never seen either of the partners in the firm of Viney and Marr: as I may have said already. On the day after the man was stabbed at our side door I saw them both.

That morning the tide was low, and Hole-in-the-Wall Stairs ended in a causeway in the midst of a little flat of gravel and mud. So, since the mud was nowhere dangerous, and there was no deep water to fall into, I was allowed to go down the steps alone and play on the foreshore while Grandfather Nat was busy with his morning's affairs; the two or three watermen lying by the causeway undertaking to keep an eye on me. And there I took my pleasure as I would, now raking in the wet pebbles, and heaving over big stones that often pulled me on to all-fours, now climbing the stairs to peep along the alley, and once or twice running as far as the bar-parlour door to report myself to Grandfather Nat, and inform him of my discoveries.

The little patch of foreshore soon rendered up all its secrets, and its area grew less by reason of the rising tide; so that I turned to other matters of interest. Out in mid-stream a cluster of lighters lay moored, waiting for the turn of the tide. Presently a little tug came puffing and fussing from somewhere alongshore, and after much shoving and hauling and shouting, scuffled off, trailing three of the lighters behind it; from which I conjectured that their loads were needed in a hurry. But the disturbance among the rest of the lighters was not done with when the tug had cleared the three from their midst; for a hawser had got foul of a rudder, and two or three men were at work with poles and hooks, recrimination and forcible words, to get things clear. Though the thing seemed no easy job; and it took my attention for some time.

But presently I tired of it, and climbed the steps to read the bills describing the people who had been found drowned. There were eleven of the bills altogether, fresh and clean; and fragments of innumerable others, older and dirtier, were round about them. Ten men and one woman had been picked up, it would seem, and all within a week or two, as I learned when I had spelled out the dates. I pored at these bills till I had read them through, being horribly fascinated by the personal marks and peculiarities so baldly set forth; the scars, the tattoo marks, the colour of the dead eyes; the clothes and boots and the contents of the pockets—though indeed most of the pockets would seem to have been empty. The woman— they guessed her age at twenty-two—wore one earring; and I entangled myself in conjectures as to what had become of the other.

I was disturbed by a shout from the causeway. I looked and saw Bill Stagg in his boat. "Is your gran'father there?" shouted Bill Stagg. "Tell him they've found his boat."

This was joyful news, and I rushed to carry it. "They've found our boat, Grandfather Nat," I cried. "Bill Stagg says so!"

Grandfather Nat was busy in the bar, and he received the information with calmness. "Ah," he said, "I knew it 'ud turn up somewhere. Bill Stagg there?" And he came out leisurely in his shirt sleeves, and stood at the head of the stairs.

"P'lice galley found your boat, cap'en," Bill Stagg reported. "You'll have to go up to the float for it."

"Right. Know where it was?"

"Up agin Elephant stairs"—Bill Stagg pointed across the river—"turned adrift and jammed among the lighters."

Grandfather Nat nodded serenely. Bill Stagg nodded in reply, shoved off from the causeway and went about his business.

The hawser was still foul among the lighters out in the stream, and a man had pulled over in a boat to help. I had told grandfather of the difficulty, and how long it had baffled the lightermen, and was asking the third of a string of questions about it all, when there was a step behind, and a voice: "Good mornin', Cap'en Nat."

My grandfather turned quickly. "Mr. Viney!" he said. "Well.... Good mornin'."

I turned also, and I was not prepossessed by Mr. Viney. His face—a face no doubt originally pale and pasty, but too long sun-burned to revert to anything but yellow in these later years of shore-life—his yellow face was ever stretched in an uneasy grin, a grin that might mean either propitiation or malice, and remained the same for both. He had the watery eyes and the goatee beard that were not uncommon among seamen, and in total I thought he much resembled one of those same hang-dog fellows that stood at corners and leaned on posts in the neighbourhood, making a mysterious living out of sailors; one of them, that is to say, in a superior suit of clothes that seemed too good for him. I suppose he may have been an inch taller than Grandfather Nat; but in the contrast between them he seemed very small and mean.

He offered his hand with a stealthy gesture, rather as though he were trying to pick my grandfather's waistcoat pocket; so that the old man stared at the hand for a moment, as if to see what he would be at, before he shook it.

"Down in the world again, Cap'en Nat," said Viney, with a shrug.

"Ay, I heard," answered Captain Nat. "I'm very sorry; but there—perhaps you'll be up again soon...."

"I come to ask you about something," Viney proceeded, as they walked away toward the bar-parlour door. "Something you'll tell me, bein' an old shipmate, if you can find out, I'm sure. Can we go into your place? No, there's a woman there."

"Only one as does washin' up an' such. I'll send her upstairs if you like."

"No, out here's best; we'll walk up and down; people get hangin' round doors an' keyholes in a place like that. Here we can see who's near us."

"What, secrets?"

"Ay." Viney gave an ugly twist to his grin. "I know some o' yours—one big un' at any rate, Cap'en Nat, don't I? So I can afford to let you into a little 'un o' mine, seein' I can't help it. Now I'd like to know if you've seen anything of Marr."

"No,—haven't seen him for months. Bolted, they tell me, an'—well you know better'n me, I expect."

"I don't know," Viney replied with emphasis. "I ought to know, but I don't. See here now. Less than a week ago he cleared

53

out, an' then I filed my petition. He might ha' been gone anywhere—bolted. Might be abroad, as would seem most likely. In plain fact he was only coming down in these parts to lie low. See? Round about here a man can lie low an' snug, an' safer than abroad, if he likes. And he had money with him—all we could get together. See?" And Viney frowned and winked, and glanced stealthily over his shoulder.

"Ah," remarked Captain Nat, drily, "I see. An' the creditors——
"

"Damn the creditors! See here, Cap'en Nat Kemp. Remember a man called Dan Webb?"

Captain Nat paled a little, and tightened his lips.

"Remember a man called Dan Webb?" Viney repeated, stopping in his walk and facing the other with the uneasy grin unchanged. "A man called Dan Webb, aboard o' the Florence along o' you an' me? 'Cause I do, anyhow. That's on'y my little hint—we're good friends altogether, o' course, Cap'en Nat; but you know what it means. Well, Marr had money with him, as I said. He was to come to a quiet anchorage hereabout, got up like a seaman, an' let me know at once."

Captain Nat, his mouth still set tight, nodded, with a grunt.

"Well, he didn't let me know. I heard nothing at all from him, an' it struck me rather of a heap to think that p'raps he'd put the double on me, an' cleared out in good earnest. But yesterday I got news. A blind fiddler chap gave me some sort o' news."

Captain Nat remembered the meeting at the street corner in the evening after the funeral. "Blind George?" he queried.

"Yes, that was all the name he gave me; a regular thick 'un, that blind chap, an' a flow o' language as would curl the sheathing off a ship's bottom. He came the evening before, it seems, but found the place shut up—servant gal took her hook. Well now, he'd done all but see Marr down here at the Blue Gate—he'd seen him as clear as a blind man could, he said, with his ears: an' he came to me to give me the tip an' earn anything I'd give him for it. It amounted to this. It was plain enough Marr had come along here all right, an' pitched on some sort o' quarters; but it was clear he wasn't fit to be trusted alone in such a place at all. For the blind chap found him drunk, an' in tow with as precious a pair o' bully-boys as Blue Gate could show. Not only drunk, neither, but drunk with a slack jaw—drunk an' gabbling, drunk an' talkin' business—my business—an' lettin' out all there was to let,—this an' that an' t'other an' Lord knows what! It was only because of his drunken jabber that the blind man found out who he was."

"And this was the day before yesterday?" asked Captain Nat.

54

"Yes."

Captain Nat shook his head. "If he was like that the day before yesterday," he said, "in tow with such chaps as you say,—well, whatever he had on him ain't on him now. An' it 'ud puzzle a cleverer man than me to find it. You may lay to that."

Viney swore, and stamped a foot, and swore again. "But see," he said, "ain't there a chance? It was in notes, all of it. Them chaps'll be afraid to pass notes. Couldn't most of it be got back on an arrangement to cash the rest? You can find 'em if you try, with all your chances. Come—I'll pay fair for what I get, to you an' all."

"See how you've left it," remarked Captain Nat; and Viney swore again. "This was all done the day before yesterday. Well, you don't hear of it yourself till yesterday, an' now you don't come to me till to-day."

Viney swore once more, and grinned twice as wide in his rage. "Yes," he said, "that was Blind George's doing. I sent him back to see what he could do, an' ain't seen him since. Like as not he's standing in with the others."

"Ay, that's likely," the old man answered, "very likely. Blind George is as tough a lot as any in Blue Gate, for all he's blind. You'd never ha' heard of it at all if they'd ha' greased him a bit at first. I expect they shut him out, to keep the plant to themselves; an' so he came to you for anything he could pick up. An' now——"

Viney cursed them all, and Blind George and himself together; but most he cursed Marr; and so talking, the two men walked to and fro in the passage.

I could see that Viney was angry, and growing angrier still. But I gave all my attention to the work at the fouled hawser. The man in the boat, working patiently with a boat-hook, succeeded suddenly and without warning, so that he almost pitched headlong into the river. The rope came up from its entanglement with a spring and a splash, flinging some amazing great object up with it, half out of water; and the men gave a cry as this thing lapsed heavily to the surface.

The man in the boat snatched his hook again and reached for the thing as it floated. Somebody threw him a length of line, and with this he made it fast to his boat, and began pulling toward the stairs, towing it. I was puzzled to guess what the object might be. It was no part of the lighter's rudder, for it lay in, rather than on, the water, and it rolled and wallowed, and seemed to tug heavily, so that the boatman had to pull his best. I wondered if he had caught some curious water-creature—a porpoise perhaps, or a seal, such as had been flung ashore in a winter storm at Blackwall a year before.

Viney and Grandfather Nat had turned their steps toward the stairs, and as they neared, my grandfather, lifting his eyes, saw the boatman and his prize, and saw the watermen leaving their boats for the foreshore. With a quick word to Viney he hastened down the stairs; and Viney himself, less interested, followed half way down, and waited.

The boatman brought up alongside the foreshore, and he and another hauled at the tow-rope. The thing in the water came in, rolling and bobbing, growing more hideously distinct as it came; it checked at the mud and stones, turned over, and with another pull lay ashore, staring and grey and streaming: a dead man.

The lips were pulled tight over the teeth, and, the hair being fair, it was the plainer to see that one side of the head and forehead was black and open with a great wound. The limbs lay limp and tumbled, all; but one leg fell aside with so loose a twist that plainly it was broken, and I heard, afterwards, that it was the leg that had caused the difficulty with the hawser.

Grandfather Nat, down at the waterside, had no sooner caught sight of the dead face than with wide eyes he turned to Viney, and shouted the one word "Look!" Then he went and took another view, longer and closer; and straightway came back in six strides to the stairs, whereon Viney was no longer standing, but sitting, his face tallowy and his grin faded.

"See him?" cried Grandfather Nat in a hushed voice. "See him! It's Marr himself, if I know him at all! Come—come and see!"

Viney pulled his arm from the old man's grasp, turned, and crawled up a stair or two. "No," he said faintly, "I—I won't, now—I—they'd know me p'raps, some of them." His breath was short, and he gulped. "Good God," he said presently, "it's him—it's him sure enough. And the clothes he had on.... But ... Cap'en—Cap'en Nat; go an' try his pockets.—Go on. There's a pocket-book—leather pocket-book.... Go on!"

"What's the good?" asked Captain Nat, with a lift of the eyebrows, and the same low voice. "What's the good? I can't fetch it away, with all them witnesses. Go yourself, an' say you're his pardner; you'd have a chance then."

"No—no. I—it ain't good enough. You know 'em; I don't. I'll stand in with you—give you a hundred if it's all there! Square 'em—you know 'em!"

"If they're to be squared you can do it as well as me. There'll be an inquest on this, an' evidence. I ain't going to be asked what I did with the man's pocket-book. No. I don't meddle in this, Mr.

56

Viney. If it ain't good enough for you to get it for yourself, it ain't good enough for me to get it for you."

"Kemp, I'll go you halves—there! Get it, an' there's four hundred for you. Eight hundred an' odd quid, in a pocket-book. Come, that's worth it, ain't it? Eight hundred an' odd quid—in a leather pocket-book! An' I'll go you halves."

Captain Nat started at the words, and stood for a moment, staring. "Eight hundred!" he repeated under his breath. "Eight hundred an' odd quid. In a leather pocket-book. Ah!" And the stare persisted, and grew thoughtful.

"Yes," replied Viney, now a little more himself. "Now you know; and it's worth it, ain't it? Don't waste time—they're turning him over themselves. You can manage all these chaps. Go on!"

"I'll see if anything's there," answered Captain Nat. "More I can't; an' if there's nothing that's an end of it."

He went down to where the men were bending over the body, to disengage the tow-line. He looked again at the drawn face under the gaping forehead, and said something to the men; then he bent and patted the soddened clothes, now here, now there; and at last felt in the breast-pocket.

Meantime Viney stood feverishly on the stairs, watching; fidgeting nervously down a step, and then down another, and then down two more. And so till Captain Nat returned.

The old man shook his head. "Cleaned out," he reported. "Cleaned out, o' course. Hit on the head an' cleaned out, like many a score better men before him, down these parts. Not a thing in the pockets anywhere. Flimped clean."

Viney's eyes were wild. "Nothing at all left?" he said. "Nothing of his own? Not a watch, nor anything?"

"No, not a watch, nor anything."

Viney stood staring at space for some moments, murmuring many oaths. Then he asked suddenly, "Where's this blind chap? Where can I find Blind George?"

Grandfather Nat shook his head. "He's all over the neighbourhood," he answered. "Try the Highway; I can't give you nearer than that."

And with no more counsel to help him, Mr. Viney was fain to depart. He went grinning and cursing up the passage and so toward the bridge, without another word or look. And when I turned to my grandfather I saw him staring fixedly at me, lost in thought, and rubbing his hand up in his hair behind, through the grey and out at the brown on top.

CHAPTER XII
IN THE CLUB-ROOM

By the side of the bills stuck at the corner of Hole-in-the-Wall Stairs—the bills that had so fascinated Stephen—a new one appeared, with the heading "Body Found." It particularised the personal marks and description of the unhappy Marr; his "fresh complexion," his brown hair, his serge suit and his anklejacks. The bill might have stood on every wall in London till it rotted, and never have given a soul who knew him a hint to guess the body his: except Viney, who knew the fact already. And the body might have been buried unidentified ere Viney would have shown himself in the business, were it not for the interference of Mr. Cripps. For industry of an unprofitable kind was a piece of Mr. Cripps's nature; and, moreover, he was so regular a visitor at the mortuary as to have grown an old friend of the keeper. His persistent prying among the ghastly liers-in-state, at first on plea of identifying a friend—a contingency likely enough, since his long-shore acquaintance was wide—and later under the name of friendly calls, was an indulgence that had helped him to consideration as a news-monger, and twice had raised him to the elevation of witness at an inquest; a distinction very gratifying to his simple vanity. He entertained high hopes of being called witness in the case of the man stabbed at the side door of the Hole in the Wall; and was scarce seen at Captain Nat's all the next day, preferring to frequent the mortuary. So it happened that he saw the other corpse that was carried thence from Hole-in-the-Wall Stairs.

"There y'are," said the mortuary-keeper. "There's a fresh 'un, just in from the river, unknown. You dunno 'im either, I expect."

But Mr. Cripps was quite sure that he did. Curious and eager, he walked up between the two dead men, his grimy little body being all that divided them in this their grisly reunion. "I do know 'im," he insisted, thoughtfully. "Leastways I've seen 'im somewheres, I'm sure." The little man gazed at the dreadful head, and then at the rafters: then shut his eyes with a squeeze that drove his nose into amazing lumps and wrinkles; then looked at the head again, and squeezed his eyelids together once more; and at last started back, his eyes rivalling his very nose itself for prominence. "Why!" he gasped, "it is! It is, s'elp me!... It's Mr. Marr, as is pardners with Mr.

58

Viney! I on'y see 'im once in my life, but I'll swear it's 'im!... Lord, what a phenomenal go!"

And with that Mr. Cripps rushed off incontinent to spread the news wherever anybody would listen. He told the police, he told the loafers, he told Captain Nat and everybody in his bar; he told the watermen at the stairs, he shouted it to the purlmen in their boats, and he wriggled into conversation with perfect strangers to tell them too. So that it came to pass that Viney, being called upon by the coroner's officer, was fain to swallow his reluctance and come forward at the inquest.

That was held at the Hole in the Wall twenty-four hours after the body had been hauled ashore. The two inquests were held together, in fact, Marr's and that of the broken-nosed man, stabbed in the passage. Two inquests, or even three, in a day, made no uncommon event in those parts, where perhaps a dozen might be held in a week, mostly ending with the same doubtful verdict— Found Drowned. But here one of the inquiries related to an open and witnessed murder, and that fact gave some touch of added interest to the proceedings.

Accordingly a drifting group hung about the doors of the Hole in the Wall at the appointed time,—just such an idle, changing group as had hung there all the evening after the man had been stabbed; and in the midst stood Blind George with his fiddle, his vacant white eye rolling upward, his mouth full of noisy ribaldry, and his fiddle playing punctuation and chorus to all he said or sang. He turned his ear at the sound of many footsteps leaving the door near him.

"There they go!" he sang out; "there they go, twelve on 'em!" And indeed it was the jury going off to view the bodies. "There they go, twelve good men an' true, an' bloomin' proud they are to fancy it! Got a copper for Blind George, gentlemen? Not a brown for pore George?... Not them; not a brass farden among the 'ole dam good an' lawful lot.... Ahoy! ain't Gubbins there,—the good an' lawful pork-butcher as 'ad to pay forty bob for shovin' a lump o' fat under the scales? Tell the crowner to mind 'is pockets!"

The idlers laughed, and one flung a copper, which Blind George snatched almost before it had fallen. "Ha! ha!" he cried, "there's a toff somewhere near, I can tell by the sound of his money! Here goes for a stave!" And straightway be broke into:—

O they call me Hanging Johnny, With my hang, boys, hang!

The mortuary stood at no great distance and soon the jury were back in the club-room over the bar, and at work on the first case. The police had had some difficulty as to identification of the

59

stabbed man. The difficulty arose not only because there were no relations in the neighbourhood to feel the loss, but as much because the persons able to make the identification kept the most distant possible terms with the police, and withheld information from them as a matter of principle. Albeit a reluctant ruffian was laid hold of who was induced sulkily to admit that he had known the deceased to speak to, and lodged near him in Blue Gate; that the deceased was called Bob Kipps; that he was quite lately come into the neighbourhood; and that he had no particular occupation, as far as witness knew. It needed some pressure to extract the information that Kipps, during the short time he was in Blue Gate, chiefly consorted with one Dan Ogle, and that witness had seen nothing of Ogle that day, nor the day before.

There was also a woman called to identify—a woman more reluctant than the man; a woman of coarse features, dull eyes, tousled hair, and thick voice, sluttish with rusty finery. Name, Margaret Flynn; though at the back of the little crowd that had squeezed into the court she was called Musky Mag. It was said there, too, that Mag, in no degree one of the fainting sort, had nevertheless swooned when taken into the mortuary—gone clean off with a flop; true, she explained it, afterward, by saying that she had only expected to see one body, but found herself brought face to face with two; and of course there was the other there—Marr's. But it was held no such odds between one corpse and two that an outer-and-outer like Mag should go on the faint over it. This was reasonable enough, for the crowd. But not for a woman who had sat to drink with three men, and in a short hour or so had fallen over the battered corpse of one of them, in the dark of her room; who had been forced, now, to view the rent body of a second, and in doing it to meet once again the other, resurrected, bruised, sodden and horrible; and who knew that all was the work of the last of the three, and that man in peril of the rope: the man, too, of all the world, in her eye....

Her evidence, given with plain anxiety and a nervous unsteadiness of the mouth, added nothing to the tale. The man was Bob Kipps; he was a stranger till lately—came, she had heard tell, from Shoreditch or Hoxton; saw him last a day or two ago: knew nothing of his death beyond what she had heard; did not know where Dan Ogle was (this very vehemently, with much shaking of the head); had not seen him with deceased—but here the police inspector handed the coroner a scribbled note, and the coroner having read it and passed it back, said no more. Musky Mag stood

60

aside; while the inspector tore the note into small pieces and put the pieces in his pocket.

Nathaniel Kemp, landlord of the house, told the story of the murder as he saw it, and of his chase of the murderer. Did not know deceased, and should be unable to identify the murderer if he met him again, having seen no more than his figure in the dark.

All this time Mr. Cripps had been standing, in eager trepidation, foremost among the little crowd, nodding and lifting his hand anxiously, strenuous to catch the coroner's officer's attention at the dismissal of each witness, and fearful lest his offer of evidence, made a dozen times before the coroner came, should be forgotten. Now at last the coroner's officer condescended to notice him, and being beckoned, Mr. Cripps swaggered forward, his greasy widewake crushed under his arm, and his face radiant with delighted importance. He bowed to the coroner, kissed the book with a flourish, and glanced round the court to judge how much of the due impression was yet visible.

The coroner signified that he was ready to hear whatever Mr. Cripps knew of this matter.

Mr. Cripps "threw a chest," stuck an arm akimbo, and raised the other with an oratorical sweep so large that his small voice, when it came, seemed all the smaller. "Hi was in the bar, sir," he piped, "the bar, sir, of this 'ouse, bein' long acquainted with an' much respectin' Cap'en Kemp, an' in the 'abit of visitin' 'ere in the intervals of the pursoot of my hart. Hem! Hi was in the bar, sir, when my attention was attracted by a sudden noise be'hind, or as I may say, in the rear of, the bar-parlour. Hi was able to distinguish, gentlemen of the jury, what might be called, in a common way o' speakin', a bump or a bang, sich as would be occasioned by an unknown murderer criminally shoving his un'appy victim's 'ed agin the back-door of a public-'ouse. Hi was able to distinguish it, sir, from a 'uman cry which follered: a 'uman cry, or as it might be, a holler, sich as would be occasioned by the un'appy victim 'avin' 'is 'ed shoved agin the back-door aforesaid. Genelmen, I 'esitated not a moment. I rushed forward."

Mr. Cripps paused so long to give the statement effect that the coroner lost patience. "Yes," he said, "you rushed forward. Do you mean you jumped over the bar?"

For a moment Mr. Cripps's countenance fell; truly it would have been more imposing to have jumped over the bar. But he was on his oath, and he must do his best with the facts. "No, sir," he explained, a little tamely, "not over the bar, but reether the opposite way, so to speak, towards the door. I rushed forward, genelmen, in a sort of rearwards direction, through the door, an' round into the alley. Immediate as I turned the corner, genelmen, I be'eld with my own eyes the unknown murderer; I see 'im a-risin' from over 'is un'appy victim, an' I see as the criminal tragedy had transpired. I—I rushed forward."

The sensation he looked for being slow in coming, another rush seemed expedient; but it fell flat as the first, and Mr. Cripps struggled on, desperately conscious that he had nothing else to say.

"I rushed forward, sir; seein' which the miscreant absconded—absconded, no doubt with—with the proceeds; an' seein' Cap'en Kemp abscondin' after him, I turned an' be'eld the un'appy victim—the corpse now in custody, sir—a-layin' in the bar-parlour, 'elpless an'—an' decimated.... I—rushed forward."

It was sad to see how little the coroner was impressed; there was even something in his face not unlike a smile; and Mr. Cripps was at the end of his resources. But if he could have seen the face of Musky Mag, in the little crowd behind him, he might have been consoled. She alone, of all who heard, had followed his rhetoric with an agony of attention, word by word: even as she had followed the earlier evidence. Now her strained face was the easier merely by contrast with itself when Mr. Cripps was in full cry; and a moment later it was tenser than ever.

"Yes, yes, Mr. Cripps," the coroner said; "no doubt you were very active, but we don't seem to have increased the evidence. You say you saw the man who stabbed the deceased in the passage. Did you know him at all? Ever see him before?"

Here, mayhap, was some chance of an effect after all. Mr. Cripps could scarce have distinguished the murderer from one of the posts in the alley; but he said, with all the significance he could give the words: "Well, sir, I won't go so far as to swear to 'is name, sir; no, sir, not to 'is name, certainly not." And therewith he made his sensation at last, bringing upon himself the twenty-four eyes of the jury all together.

The coroner looked up sharply. "Oh," he said, "you know him by sight then? Does he belong to the neighbourhood?"

Now it was not Mr. Cripps who had said he knew the murderer by sight, but the coroner. Far be it from him, thought the aspirant for fame, to contradict the coroner, and so baulk himself of the credit thus thrust upon him. So he answered with the same cautious significance and a succession of portentous nods. "Your judgment, sir, is correct; quite correct."

"Come then, this is important. You would be able to recognise him again, of course?"

There was no retreat—Mr. Cripps was in for it. It was an unforeseen consequence of the quibble, but since plunge he must he plunged neck and crop. "I'd know 'im anywhere," he said triumphantly.

There was an odd sound in the crowd behind, and a fall. Captain Nat strode across, and the crowd wondered; for Musky Mag had fainted again.

The landlord lifted her, and carried her to the stairs. When the door had closed behind them, and the coroner's officer had shouted the little crowd into silence, the inquest took a short course to its end.

Mr. Cripps, in the height of his consequence, began to feel serious misgivings as to the issue of his stumble beyond the verities; and the coroner's next words were a relief.

"I think that will be enough, Mr. Cripps," the coroner said; "no doubt the police will be glad of your assistance." And with that he gave the jury the little summing up that the case needed. There was the medical evidence, and the evidence of the stabbing, and that evidence pointed to an unmistakable conclusion. Nobody was in custody, nor had the murderer been positively identified, and such evidence as there was in this respect was for the consideration of the police. He thought the jury would have no difficulty in arriving at a verdict. The jury had none; and the verdict was Murder by some Person or Persons unknown.

The other inquest gave even less trouble. Mr. Henry Viney, shipowner, had seen the body, and identified it as that of his partner Lewis Marr. Marr had suddenly disappeared a week ago, and an examination of his accounts showed serious defalcations, in consequence of which witness had filed his petition in bankruptcy. Whether or not Marr had taken money with him witness could not say, as deceased had entire charge of the accounts; but it seemed more likely that embezzlement had been going on for some time past, and Marr had fled when detection could no longer be averted. This might account for his dressing, and presumably seeking work, as a sailor.

The divisional surgeon of police had examined the body, and found a large wound on the head, fully sufficient to have caused death, inflicted either by some heavy, blunt instrument, or by a fall from a height on a hard substance. One thigh was fractured, and there were other wounds and contusions, but these, as well as the broken thigh, were clearly caused after death. The blow on the head might have been caused by an accident on the riverside, or it might have been inflicted wilfully by an assailant.

63

Then there was the evidence of the man who had found the body foul of a rudder and a hawser, and of the police who had found nothing on the body. And there was no more evidence at all. The coroner having sympathised deeply with Mr. Viney, gave the jury the proper lead, and the jury with perfect propriety returned the open verdict that the doctor's evidence and the coroner's lead suggested. The case, except for the circumstances of Marr's flight, was like a hundred others inquired upon thereabout in the course of a few weeks, and in an hour it was in a fair way to be forgotten, even by the little crowd that clumped downstairs to try both cases all over again in the bar of the Hole in the Wall.

To the coroner, the jury, and the little crowd, these were two inquests with nothing to connect them but the accident of time and the convenience of the Hole in the Wall club-room. But Blind George, standing in the street with his fiddle, and getting the news from the club-room in scraps between song and patter, knew more and guessed better.

CHAPTER XIII
STEPHEN'S TALE

I found it a busy morning at the Hole in the Wall, that of the two inquests. I perceived that, by some occult understanding, business in one department was suspended; the pale man idled without, and nobody came into the little compartment to exhibit valuables. Grandfather Nat had a deal to do in making ready the club-room over the bar, and then in attending the inquests. And it turned out that Mrs. Grimes had settled on this day in particular to perform a vast number of extra feats of housewifery in the upper floors. Notwithstanding the disturbance of this additional work, Mrs. Grimes was most amazingly amiable, even to me; but she was so persistent in requiring, first the key of one place, then of another, next of a chest of drawers, and again of a cupboard, that at last my grandfather distractedly gave her the whole bunch, and told her not to bother him any more. The bunch held all she could require—indeed I think it comprised every key my grandfather had, except that of his cash-box—and she went away with it amiable still, notwithstanding the hastiness of his expressions; so that I was

64

amazed to find Mrs. Grimes so meek, and wondered vaguely and childishly if it were because she felt ill, and expected to die shortly.

Mr. Cripps was in the bar as soon as the doors were open, in a wonderful state of effervescence. He was to make a great figure at the inquest, it appeared, and the pride and glory of it kept him nervously on the strut, till the coroner came, and Mr. Cripps mounted to the club-room with the jury. He was got up for his part as completely as circumstances would allow; grease was in his hair, his hat stood at an angle, and his face exhibited an unfamiliar polish, occasioned by a towel.

For my own part, I sat in the bar-parlour and amused myself as I might. Blind George was singing in the street, and now and again I could hear the guffaw that signalised some sally that had touched his audience. Above, things were quiet enough for some while, and then my grandfather came heavily downstairs carrying a woman who had fainted. I had not noticed the woman among the people who went up, but now Grandfather Nat brought her through the bar, and into the parlour; and as she lay on the floor just as the stabbed man had lain, I recognised her face also; for she was the coarse-faced woman who had stopped my grandfather near Blue Gate with vague and timid questions, when we were on our way from the London Dock.

Grandfather Nat roared up the little staircase for Mrs. Grimes, and presently she descended, amiable still; till she saw the coarse woman, and was asked to help her. She looked on the woman with something of surprise and something of confusion; but carried it off at once with a toss of the head, a high phrase or so—"likes of 'er—respectable woman"—and a quick retreat upstairs.

I believe my grandfather would have brought her down again by main force, but the woman on the floor stirred, and began scrambling up, even before she knew where she was. She held the shelf, and looked dully about her, with a hoarse "Beg pardon, sir, beg pardon." Then she went across toward the door, which stood ajar, stared stupidly, with a look of some dawning alarm, and said again, "Beg pardon, sir—I bin queer"; and with that was gone into the passage.

It was not long after her departure ere the business above was over, and the people came tramping and talking down into the bar, filling it close, and giving Joe the potman all the work he could do. The coroner came down by our private stairs into the bar-parlour, ushered with great respect by my grandfather; and at his heels, taking occasion by a desperately extemporised conversation with Grandfather Nat, came Mr. Cripps.

There had never been an inquest at the Hole in the Wall before, and my grandfather had been at some exercise of mind as to the proper entertainment of the coroner. He had decided, after consideration, that the gentleman could scarce be offended at the offer of a little lunch, and to that end he had made ready with a cold fowl and a bottle of claret, which Mrs. Grimes would presently be putting on the table. The coroner was not offended, but he would take no lunch; he was very pleasantly obliged by the invitation, but his lunch had been already ordered at some distance; and so he shook hands with Grandfather Nat and went his way. A circumstance that had no small effect on my history.

For it seemed to Mr. Cripps, who saw the coroner go, that by dexterous management the vacant place at our dinner-table (for what the coroner would call lunch we called dinner) might fall to himself. It had happened once or twice before, on special occasions, that he had been allowed to share a meal with Captain Nat, and now that he was brushed and oiled for company, and had publicly distinguished himself at an inquest, he was persuaded that the occasion was special beyond precedent, and he set about to improve it with an assiduity and an innocent cunning that were very transparent indeed. So he was affectionately admiring with me, deferentially loquacious with my grandfather, and very friendly with Joe the potman and Mrs. Grimes. It was a busy morning, he observed, and he would be glad to do anything to help.

At that time the houses on Wapping Wall were not encumbered with dust-bins, since the river was found a more convenient receptacle for rubbish. Slops were flung out of a back window, and kitchen refuse went the same way, or was taken to the river stairs and turned out, either into the water or on the foreshore, as the tide might chance. Mrs. Grimes carried about with her in her dustings and sweepings an old coal-scuttle, which held hearth-bushes, shovels, ashes, cinders, potato-peelings, and the like; and at the end of her work, when the brushes and shovels had been put away, she carried the coal-scuttle, sometimes to the nearest window, but more often to the river stairs, and flung what remained into the Thames.

Just as Mr. Cripps was at his busiest and politest, Mrs. Grimes appeared with the old coal-scuttle, piled uncommonly high with ashes and dust and half-burned pipe-lights. She set it down by the door, gave my grandfather his keys, and turned to prepare the table. Instantly Mr. Cripps, watchful in service, pounced on the scuttle.

"I'll pitch this 'ere away for you, mum," he said, "while you're seein' to Cap'en Kemp's dinner"; and straightway started for the stairs.

Mrs. Grimes's back was turned at the moment, and this gave Mr. Cripps the start of a yard or two; but she flung round and after him like a maniac; so that both Grandfather Nat and I stared in amazement.

"Give me that scuttle!" she cried, snatching at the hinder handle. "Mind your own business, an' leave my things alone!"

Mr. Cripps was amazed also, and he stuttered, "I—I—I—on'y—on'y——"

"Drop it, you fool!" the woman hissed, so suddenly savage that Mr. Cripps did drop it, with a start that sent him backward against a post; and the consequence was appalling.

Mr. Cripps was carrying the coal-scuttle by its top handle, and Mrs. Grimes, reaching after it, had seized that at the back; so that when Mr. Cripps let go, everything in the scuttle shot out on the paving-stones; first, of course, the ashes and the pipe-lights; then on the top of them, crowning the heap—Grandfather Nat's cash-box!

I suppose my grandfather must have recovered from his astonishment first, for the next thing I remember is that he had Mrs. Grimes back in the bar-parlour, held fast by the arm, while he carried his cash-box in the disengaged hand. Mr. Cripps followed, bewildered but curious; and my grandfather, pushing his prisoner into a far corner, turned and locked the door.

Mrs. Grimes, who had been crimson, was now white; but more, it seemed to me, with fury than with fear. My grandfather took the key from his watchguard and opened the box, holding it where the contents were visible to none but himself. He gave no more than a quick glance within, and re-locked it; from which I judged—and judged aright—that the pocket-book was safe.

"There's witnesses enough here," said my grandfather,—for Joe the potman was now staring in from the bar—"to give you a good dose o' gaol, mum. 'Stead o' which I pay your full week's money and send you packin'!" He pulled out some silver from his pocket. "Grateful or not to me don't matter, but I hope you'll be honest where you go next, for your own sake."

"Grateful! Honest!" Mrs. Grimes gasped, shaking with passion. "'Ear 'im talk! Honest! Take me to the station now, and bring that box an' show 'em inside it! Go on!"

I felt more than a little alarmed at this challenge, having regard to the history of the pocket-book; and I remembered the night when we first examined it, the creaking door, and the soft sounds on the stairs. But Grandfather Nat was wholly undisturbed;

he counted over the money calmly, and pushed it across the little table.

"There it is, mum," he said, "an' there's your bonnet an' shawl in the corner. There's nothing else o' yours in the place, I believe, so there's no need for you to go out o' my sight till you go out of it altogether. That you'd better do quick. I'll lay the dinner myself."

Mrs. Grimes swept up the money and began fixing her bonnet on her head and tying the strings under her chin, with savage jerks and a great play of elbow; her lips screwing nervously, and her eyes blazing with spite.

"Ho yus!" she broke out—though her rage was choking her—as she snatched her shawl. "Ho yus! A nice pusson, Cap'en Nat Kemp, to talk about honesty an' gratefulness—a nice pusson! A nice teacher for young master 'opeful, I must say, an' 'opin' 'e'll do ye credit! It ain't the last you'll see o' me, Captain Nat Kemp!... Get out o' my way, you old lickspittle!"

Mr. Cripps got out of it with something like a bound, and Mrs. Grimes was gone with a flounce and a slam of the door.

Scold as she was, and furious as she was, I was conscious that something in my grandfather's scowl had kept her speech within bounds, and shortened her clamour; for few cared to face Captain Nat's anger. But with the slam of the door the scowl broke, and he laughed.

"Come," he said, "that's well over, an' I owe you a turn, Mr. Cripps, though you weren't intending it. Stop an' have a bit of dinner. And if you'd like something on account to buy the board for the sign—or say two boards if you like—we'll see about it after dinner."

It will be perceived that Grandfather Nat had no reason to regret the keeping of his cash-box key on his watchguard. For had it been with the rest, in Mrs. Grimes's hands, she need never have troubled to smuggle out the box among the ashes, since the pocket-book was no such awkward article, and would have gone in her pocket. Mrs. Grimes had taken her best chance and failed. The disorders caused by the inquests had left her unobserved, the keys were in her hands, and the cash-box was left in the cupboard upstairs; but the sedulous Mr. Cripps had been her destruction.

As for that artist, he attained his dinner, and a few shillings under the name of advance; and so was well pleased with his morning's work.

68

CHAPTER XIV
STEPHEN'S TALE

A policeman brought my grandfather a bill, which was stuck against the bar window with gelatines; and just such another bill was posted on the wall at the head of Hole-in-the-Wall Stairs, above the smaller bills that advertised the found bodies. This new bill was six times the size of those below; it was headed "Murder" in grim black capitals, and it set forth an offer of fifty pounds reward for information which should lead to the apprehension of the murderer of Robert Kipps.

The offer gave Grandfather Nat occasion for much solemn banter of Mr. Cripps; banter which seemed to cause Mr. Cripps a curious uneasiness, and time and again stopped his eloquence in full flood. He had been at the pains to cut from newspapers such reports of the inquest as were printed; and though they sadly disappointed him by their brevity, and all but two personally affronted him by disregarding his evidence and himself altogether, still he made great play with the exceptional two, in the bar. But he was quick to drop the subject when Captain Nat urged him in pursuit of the reward.

"Come," my grandfather would say, "you're neglecting your fortune, you know. There's fifty pound waitin' for you to pick up, if you'd only go an' collar that murderer. An' you'd know him anywhere." Whereupon Mr.

Cripps would look a little frightened, and subside.

I did not learn till later how the little painter's vanity had pushed him over bounds at the inquest, so far that he committed himself to an absolute recognition of the murderer. The fact alarmed him not a little, on his return to calmness, and my grandfather, who understood his indiscretion as well as himself, and enjoyed its consequences, in his own grim way, amused himself at one vacant moment and another by setting Mr. Cripps's alarm astir again.

"You're throwing away your luck," he would say, perhaps, "seein' you know him so well by sight. If you're too well-off to bother about fifty pound, give some of us poor 'uns a run for it, an' put us on to him. I wish I'd been able to see him so clear." For in truth Grandfather Nat well knew that nobody had had so near a chance of seeing the murderer's face as himself; and that Mr. Cripps, at the top of the passage—perhaps even round the corner—had no chance at all.

It was because of Mr. Cripps's indiscretion, in fact—this I learned later still—that the police were put off the track of the real criminal. For after due reflection on the direful complications whereinto his lapse promised to fling him, that distinguished witness, as I have already hinted, fell into a sad funk. So, though he needs must hold to the tale that he knew the man by sight, and could recognise him again, he resolved that come what might, he would identify nobody, and so keep clear of further entanglements. Now the police suspicions fell shrewdly on Dan Ogle, a notorious ruffian of the neighbourhood. He had been much in company of the murdered man of late, and now was suddenly gone from his accustomed haunts. Moreover, there was the plain agitation of the woman he consorted with, Musky Mag, at the inquest: she had fainted, indeed, when Mr. Cripps had been so positive about identifying the murderer. These things were nothing of evidence, it was true; for that they must depend on the witness who saw the fellow's face, knew him by sight, and could identify him. But when they came to this witness with their inquiries and suggestions the thing went overboard at a breath. Was the assassin a tall man? Not at all—rather short, in fact. Was he a heavy-framed, bony fellow? On the contrary, he was fat rather than bony. Did Mr. Cripps ever happen to have seen a man called Dan Ogle, and was this man at all like him? Mr. Cripps had been familiar with Dan Ogle's appearance from his youth up (this was true, for the painter's acquaintance was wide and diverse) but the man who killed Bob Kipps was as unlike him as it was possible for any creature on two legs to be. Then, would Mr. Cripps, if the thing came to trial, swear that the man he saw was not Dan Ogle? Mr. Cripps was most fervently and desperately ready and anxious to swear that it was not, and could not by any possibility be Dan Ogle, or anybody like him.

This brought the police inquiries to a fault; even had their suspicions been stronger and better supported, it would have been useless to arrest Dan Ogle, supposing they could find him; for this, the sole possible witness to identity, would swear him innocent. So they turned their inquiries to fresh quarters, looking among the waterside population across the river—since it was plain that the murderer had rowed over—for recent immigrants from Wapping. For a little while Mr. Cripps was vexed and disquieted with invitations to go with a plain-clothes policeman and "take a quiet look" at some doubtful characters; but of course with no result, beyond the welcome one of an occasional free drink ordered as an excuse for waiting at bars and tavern-corners; and in time these attentions ceased, for the police were reduced to waiting for evidence to turn up; and Mr. Cripps breathed freely once more. While Dan Ogle remained undisturbed, and justice was balked for a while; for it turned out in the end that when the police suspected Dan Ogle they were right, and when they went to other conjectures they were wrong.

All this was ahead of my knowledge at the moment, however, as, indeed, it is somewhat ahead of my story; and for the while I did no more than wonder to see Mr. Cripps abashed at an encouragement to earn fifty pounds; for he seemed not a penny richer than before, and still impetrated odd coppers on account of the signboard of promise.

Once or twice we saw Mr. Viney, and on each occasion he borrowed money off Grandfather Nat. The police were about the house a good deal at this time, because of the murder, or I think he might have come oftener. The first time he came I heard him telling my grandfather that he had got hold of Blind George, that Blind George had told him a good deal about the missing money, and that with his help he hoped for a chance of saving some of it. He added, mysteriously, that it had been "nearer hereabouts than you might think, at one time"; a piece of news that my grandfather received with a proper appearance of surprise. But was it safe to confide in Blind George? Viney swore for answer, and said that the rascal had stipulated for such a handsome share that it would pay him to play square.

On the last of these visits I again overheard some scraps of their talk, and this time it was angrier. I judged that Viney wanted more money than my grandfather was disposed to give him. They were together in the back room where the boxes and bottles were— the room into which I had seen Bill Stagg's head and shoulders thrust by way of the trap-door. My grandfather's voice was low, and from time to time he seemed to be begging Viney to lower his; so that I wondered to find Grandfather Nat so mild, since in the bar he never twice told a man to lower his voice, but if once were not enough, flung him into the street. And withal Viney paid no heed, but talked as he would, so that I could catch his phrases again and again.

"Let them hush as is afraid—I ain't," he said. And again: "O, am I? Not me.... It's little enough for me, if it does; not the rope, anyway." And later, "Yes, the rope, Cap'en Kemp, as you know well enough; the rope at Newgate Gaol.... Dan Webb, aboard o' the Florence.... The Florence that was piled up on the Little Dingoes in

71

broad day.... As you was ordered o' course, but that don't matter.... That's what I want now, an' no less. Think it lucky I offer to pay back when I get—... Well, be sensible—... I'm friendly enough.... Very well."

Presently my grandfather, blacker than common about brow and eyes, but a shade paler in the cheek, came into the bar-parlour and opened the trade cash-box—not the one that Mrs. Grimes had hidden among the cinders, but a smaller one used for gold and silver. He counted out a number of sovereigns—twenty, I believe— put the box away, and returned to the back room. And in a few minutes, with little more talk, Mr. Viney was gone.

Grandfather Nat came into the bar-parlour again, and his face cleared when he saw me, as it always would, no matter how he had been ruffled. He stood looking in my face for a little, but with the expression of one whose mind is engaged elsewhere. Then he rubbed his hand on my head, and said abstractedly, and rather to himself, I fancied, than to me: "Never mind, Stevy; we got it back beforehand, forty times over." A remark that I thought over afterward, in bed, with the reflection that forty times twenty was eight hundred.

But Mr. Viney's talk in the back room brought most oddly into my mind, in a way hard to account for, the first question I put to my grandfather after my arrival at the Hole in the Wall: "Did you ever kill a man, Grandfather Nat?"

CHAPTER XV
STEPHEN'S TALE

The repeated multiplication of twenty by forty sent me to sleep that night, and I woke with that arithmetical exercise still running in my head. A candle was alight in the room—ours was one of several houses in Wapping Wall without gas—and I peeped sleepily over the bed-clothes. Grandfather Nat was sitting with the cash-box on his knees, and the pocket-book open in his hand. He may just have been counting the notes over again, or not; but now he was staring moodily at the photograph that lay with them. Once or twice he turned his eyes aside, and then back again to the picture, as though searching his memory for some old face; then I thought he would toss it away as something valueless; but when his glance fell on the fireless grate he returned the card to its place and locked the box.

When the cash-box was put away in the little cupboard at his bed-head, he came across and looked down at me. At first I shut my eyes, but peeped. I found him looking on me with a troubled and thoughtful face; so that presently I sat up with a jump and asked him what he was thinking about.

"Fox's sleep, Stevy?" he said, with his hand under my chin. "Well, boy, I was thinking about you. I was thinking it's a good job your father's coming home soon, Stevy; though I don't like parting with you."

Parting with me? I did not understand. Wouldn't father be going away again soon?

"Well, I dunno, Stevy, I dunno. I've been thinking a lot just lately, that's a fact. This place is good enough for me, but it ain't a good place to bring up a boy like you in; not to make him the man I want you to be, Stevy. Somehow it didn't strike me that way at first, though it ought to ha' done. It ought to ha' done, seein' it struck strangers—an' not particular moral strangers at that."

He was thinking of Blind George and Mrs. Grimes. Though at the moment I wondered if his talk with Mr. Viney had set him doubting.

"No, Stevy," he resumed, "it ain't giving you a proper chance, keeping you here. You can't get lavender water out o' the bilge, an' this part's the bilge of all London. I want you to be a better man than me, Stevy."

I could not imagine anybody being a better man than Grandfather Nat, and the prospect of leaving him oppressed me dismally. And where was I to go? I remembered the terrible group of aunts at my mother's funeral, and a shadowy fear that I might be transferred to one of those virtuous females—perhaps to Aunt Martha—put a weight on my heart. "Don't send me away, Gran'fa Nat!" I pleaded, with something pulling at the corners of my mouth; "I haven't been a bad boy yet, have I?"

He caught me up and sat me on his fore-arm, so that my face almost touched his, and I could see my little white reflection in his eyes. "You're the best boy in England, Stevy," he said, and kissed me affectionately. "The best boy in the world. An' I wouldn't let go o' you for a minute but for your own good. But see now, Stevy, see; as to goin' away, now. You'll have to go to school, my boy, won't you? An' the best school we can manage—a gentleman's school; boardin' school, you know. Well, that'll mean goin' away, won't it? An' then it wouldn't do for you to go to a school like that, not from here, you know—which you'll understand when you get there, among the others. My boy—my boy an' your father's—has got to be as good a gentleman as any of 'em, an' not looked down on because o' comin' from a Wapping public like this, an' sent by a rough old chap like me. See?"

I thought very hard over this view of things, which was difficult to understand. Who should look down on me because of Grandfather Nat, of whom I was so fond and so proud? Grandfather Nat, who had sailed ships all over the world, had seen storms and icebergs and wrecks, and who was treated with so much deference by everybody who came to the Hole in the Wall? Then I thought again of the aunts at the funeral, and remembered how they had tilted their chins at him; and I wondered, with forebodings, if people at a boarding school were like those aunts.

"So I've been thinking, Stevy, I've been thinking," my grandfather went on, after a pause. "Now, there's the wharf on the Cop. The work's gettin' more, and Grimes is gettin' older. But you don't know about the wharf. Grimes is the man that manages there for me; he's Mrs. Grimes's brother-in-law, an' when his brother died he recommended the widder to me, an' that's how she came: an' now she's gone; but that's neither here nor there. Years ago Grimes himself an' a boy was enough for all the work there was; now there's three men reg'lar, an' work for more. Most o' the lime comes off the barges there for the new gas-works, an' more every week. Now there's business there, an' a respectable business—too much for Grimes. An' if your father'll take on a shore job—an' it's a hard life, the sea—here it is. He can have a share—have the lot if he likes—for your sake, Stevy; an' it'll build up into a good thing. Grimes'll be all right—we can always find a job for him. An' you can go an' live with your father somewhere respectable an' convenient; not such a place as Wapping, an' not such people. An' you can go to school from there, like any other young gentleman. We'll see about it when your father comes home."

"But shan't I ever see you, Gran'fa' Nat?"

"See me, my boy? Ay, that you will—if you don't grow too proud—that you will, an' great times we'll have, you an' your father an' me, all ashore together, in the holidays, won't we? An' I'll take care of your own little fortune—the notes—till you're old enough to have it. I've been thinking about that, too." Here he stood me on my bed and playfully pushed me back and forward by the shoulders. "I've been thinking about that, an' if it was lyin' loose in the street I'd be puzzled clean to say who'd really lost it, what with one thing

74

an' another. But it ain't in the street, an' it's yours, with no puzzle about it. But there—lie down, Stevy, an' go to sleep. Your old grandfather's holdin' forth worse'n a parson, eh? Comes o' bein' a lonely man an' havin' nobody to talk to, except myself, till you come. Lie down an' don't bother yourself. We must wait till your father comes home. We'll keep watch for the Juno in the List,—she ought to ha' been reported at Barbadoes before this. An' we must run down to Blackwall, too, an' see if there's any letters from him. So go to sleep now, Stevy—we'll settle it all—we'll settle it all when your father comes home!"

So I lay and dozed, with words to send me to sleep instead of figures: till they made a tune and seemed to dance to it. "When father comes home: when father comes home: we'll settle it all, when father comes home!" And presently, in some unaccountable way, Mr. Cripps came into the dance with his "Up to their r'yals, up to their r'yals: the wessels is deep in, up to their r'yals!" and so I fell asleep wholly.

In the morning I was astir early, and watching the boats and the shipping from the bedroom window ere my grandfather had ceased his alarming snore. It was half an hour later, and Grandfather Nat was busy with his razor on the upper lip that my cheeks so well remembered, when we heard Joe the potman at the street door. Whereat I took the keys and ran down to let him in; a feat which I accomplished by aid of a pair of steps, much tugging at heavy bolts, and a supreme wrench at the big key.

Joe brought Lloyd's List in with him every morning from the early newsagent's in Cable Street. I took the familiar journal at once, and dived into the midst of its quaint narrow columns, crowded with italics, in hope of news from Barbadoes. For I wished to find for myself, and run upstairs, with a child's importance, to tell Grandfather Nat. But there was no news from Barbadoes—that is, there was no news of my father's ship. The name Barbadoes stood boldly enough, with reports below it, of arrivals and sailings, and one of an empty boat washed ashore; but that was all. So I sat where I was, content to wait, and to tell Grandfather Nat presently, offhand from over my paper, like a politician in the bar, that there was no news. Thus, cutting the leaves with a table-knife, my mind on my father's voyage, it occurred to me that I could not spell La Guaira, the name of the port his ship was last reported from; and I turned the paper to look for it. The name was there, with only one message attached, and while I was slowly conning the letters over for the third time, I was suddenly aware of a familiar word

75

beneath—the name of the Juno herself. And this was the notice that I read:

La Guaira, Sep. 1.

The Juno (brig) of London, Beecher, from this for Barbadoes, foundered N of Margarita. Total loss. All crew saved except first mate. Master and crew landed Margarita.

CHAPTER XVI
STEPHEN'S TALE

I cannot remember how I reached Grandfather Nat. I must have climbed the stairs, and I fancy I ran into him on the landing; but I only remember his grim face, oddly grey under the eyes, as he sat on his bed and took the paper in his hand. I do not know even what I said, and I doubt if I knew then; the only words present to my mind were "all crew saved except first mate"; and very likely that was what I said.

My grandfather drew me between his knees, and I stood with his arm about me and his bowed head against my cheek. I noticed bemusedly that with his hair fresh-brushed the line between the grey and the brown at the back was more distinct than common; and when there was a sudden clatter in the bar below I wondered if Joe had smashed something, or if it were only a tumble of the pewters. So we were for a little; and then Grandfather Nat stood up with a sound between a sigh and a gulp, looking strangely askant at me, as though it surprised him to find I was not crying. For my part I was dimly perplexed to see that neither was he; though the grey was still under his eyes, and his face seemed pinched and older. "Come, Stevy," he said, and his voice was like a groan; "we'll have the house shut again."

I cannot remember that he spoke to me any more for an hour, except to ask if I would eat any breakfast, which I did with no great loss of appetite; though indeed I was trying very hard to think, hindered by an odd vacancy of mind that made a little machine of me.

Breakfast done, my grandfather sent Joe for a cab to take us to Blackwall. I was a little surprised at the unaccustomed conveyance, and rather pleased. When we were ready to go, we found Mr. Cripps and two other regular frequenters of the bar waiting outside. I think Mr. Cripps meant to have come forward with some prepared condolence; but he stopped short when he saw my grandfather's face, and stood back with the others. The four-wheeler was a wretched vehicle, reeking of strong tobacco and stale drink; for half the employment of such cabs as the neighbourhood possessed was to carry drunken sailors, flush of money, who took bottles and pipes with them everywhere.

Whether it was the jolting of the cab—Wapping streets were paved with cobbles—that shook my faculties into place; whether it was the association of the cab and the journey to Blackwall that reminded me of my mother's funeral; or whether it was the mere lapse of a little time, I cannot tell. But as we went, the meaning of the morning's news grew on me, and I realised that my father was actually dead, drowned in the sea, and that I was wholly an orphan; and it struck me with a sense of self-reproach that the fact afflicted me no more than it did. When my mother and my little brother had died I had cried myself sodden and faint; but now, heavy of heart as I was, I felt curiously ashamed that Grandfather Nat should see me tearless. True, I had seen very little of my father, but when he was at home he was always as kind to me as Grandfather Nat himself, and led me about with him everywhere; and last voyage he had brought me a little boomerang, and only laughed when I hove it through a window that cost him three shillings. Thus I pondered blinkingly in the cab; and I set down my calmness to the reflection that my mother would have him always with her now, and be all the happier in heaven for it; for she always cried when he went to sea.

So at last we came in sight of the old quay, and had to wait till the bridge should swing behind a sea-beaten ship, with her bulwarks patched with white plank, and the salt crust thick on her spars. I could see across the lock the three little front windows of our house, shut close and dumb; and I could hear the quick chanty from the quay, where the capstan turned:—

O, I served my time on the Black Ball Line, Hurrah for the Black Ball Line! From the South Sea north to the sixty-nine, Hurrah for the Black Ball Line!

And somehow with that I cried at last.

The ship passed in, the bridge shut, and the foul old cab rattled till it stopped before the well-remembered door. The house had been closed since my mother was buried, Grandfather Nat paying the rent and keeping the key on my father's behalf; and now the door opened with a protesting creak and a shudder, and the air within was close and musty.

There were two letters on the mat, where they had fallen from the letter-flap, and both were from my father, as was plain from the writing. We carried them into the little parlour, where last we had sat with the funeral party, and my grandfather lifted the blind and flung open the window. Then he sat and put one letter on each knee.

"Stevy," he said, and again his voice was like a groan; "look at them postmarks. Ain't one Belize?"

Yes, one was Belize, the other La Guaira; and both for my mother.

"Ah, one's been lyin' here; the other must ha' come yesterday, by the same mail as brought the news." He took the two letters again, turned them over and over, and shook his head. Then he replaced them on his knees and rested his fists on his thighs, just above where they lay.

"I don't know as we ought to open 'em, Stevy," he said wearily. "I dunno, Stevy, I dunno."

He turned each over once more, and shut his fists again. "I dunno, I dunno.... Man an' wife, between 'emselves.... Wouldn't do it, living.... Stevy boy, we'll take 'em home an' burn 'em."

But to me the suggestion seemed incomprehensible—even shocking. I could see no reason for burning my father's last message home. "Perhaps there's a little letter for me, Gran'father Nat," I said. "He used to put one in sometimes. Can't we look? And mother used to read me her letters too."

My grandfather sat back and rubbed his hand up through his hair behind, as he would often do when in perplexity. At last he said, "Well, well, it's hard to tell. We should never know what we'd burnt, if we did.... We'll look, Stevy.... An' I'll read no further than I need. Come, the Belize letter's first.... Send I ain't doin' wrong, that's all."

He tore open the cover and pulled out the sheets of flimsy foreign note-paper, holding them to the light almost at arm's length, as long-sighted men do. And as he read, slowly as always, with a leathery forefinger following the line, the grey under the old man's eyes grew wet at last, and wetter. What the letter said is no matter here. There was talk of me in it, and talk of my little brother—or sister, as it might have been for all my father could know. And again there was the same talk in the second letter—the one from La Guaira. But in this latter another letter was enclosed, larger than that for my mother, which was in fact uncommonly short. And here, where the dead spoke to the dead no more, but to the living, was matter that disturbed my grandfather more than all the rest.

The enclosure was not for me, as I had hoped, but for Grandfather Nat himself; and it was not a simple loose sheet folded in with the rest, but a letter in its own smaller envelope, close shut down, with the words "Capn. Kemp" on the face. My grandfather read the first few lines with increasing agitation, and then called me to the window.

"See here, Stevy," he said, "it's wrote small, to get it in, an' I'm slow with it. Read it out quick as you can."

And so I read the letter, which I keep still, worn at the folds and corners by the old man's pocket, where he carried it afterward.

Dear Father,—Just a few lines private hoping they find you well. This is my hardest trip yet, and the queerest, and I write in case anything happens and I don't see you again. This is for yourself, you understand, and I have made it all cheerful to the Mrs., specially as she is still off her health, no doubt. Father, the Juno was not meant to come home this trip, and if ever she rounds Blackwall Point again it will be in spite of the skipper. He had his first try long enough back, on the voyage out, and it was then she was meant to go; for she was worse found than ever I saw a ship—even a ship of Viney's; and not provisioned for more than half the run out, proper rations. And I say it plain, and will say it as plain to anybody, that the vessel would have been piled up or dropped under and the insurance paid months before you get this if I had not pretty nigh mutinied more than once. He said he would have me in irons, but he shan't have the chance if I can help it. You know Beecher. Four times I reckon he has tried to pile her up, every time in the best weather and near a safe port—foreign. The men would have backed me right through—some of them did—but they deserted one after another all round the coast, Monte Video, Rio and Bahia, and small blame to them, and we filled up with half-breeds and such. The last of the ten and the boy went at Bahia, so that now I have no witness but the second mate, and he is either in it or a fool—I think a fool: but perhaps both. Not a man to back me. Else I might have tried to report or something, at Belize, though that is a thing best avoided of course. No doubt he has got his orders, so I am not to blame him, perhaps. But I have got no orders—not to lose the ship, I mean—and so I am doing my duty. Twice I have come up and took the helm from him, but that was with the English crew aboard. He has been quiet lately, and perhaps he has given the job up; at any rate I expect he won't try to pile her up again—more likely a quiet turn below with a big auger. He is still mighty particular about the long-boat being all right, and the falls clear, etc. If he does it I have a notion it may be some time when I have turned in; I can't keep awake all watches. And he knows I am about the only man aboard who won't sign whatever he likes before a consul. You know what I

79

mean; and you know Beecher too. Don't tell the Mrs. of course. Say this letter is about a new berth or what not. No doubt it is all right, but it came in my head to drop you a line, on the off chance, and a precious long line I have made of it. So no more at present from— Your Affectionate Son,

Nathaniel.

P.S. I am in half a mind to go ashore at Barbadoes, and report. But perhaps best not. That sort of thing don't do.

While I read, my grandfather had been sitting with his head between his hands, and his eyes directed to the floor, so that I could not see his face. So he remained for a little while after I had finished, while I stood in troubled wonder. Then he looked up, his face stern and hard beyond the common: and his was a stern face at best.

"Stevy," he said, "do you know what that means, that you've been a-readin'?"

I looked from his face to the letter, and back again. "It means—means ... I think the skipper sank the ship on purpose."

"It means Murder, my boy, that's what it means. Murder, by the law of England! 'Feloniously castin' away an' destroyin';' that's what they call the one thing, though I'm no lawyer-man. An' it means prison; though why, when a man follows orders faithful, I can't say; but well I know it. An' if any man loses his life thereby it's Murder, whether accidental or not; Murder an' the Rope, by the law of England, an' bitter well I know that too! O bitter well I know it!"

He passed his palm over his forehead and eyes, and for a moment was silent. Then he struck the palm on his knee and broke forth afresh.

"Murder, by the law of England, even if no more than accident in God's truth. How much the more then this here, when the one man as won't stand and see it done goes down in his berth? O, I've known that afore, too, with a gimlet through the door-frame; an' I know Beecher. But orders is orders, an' it's them as gives them as is to reckon with. I've took orders myself.... Lord! Lord! an' I've none but a child to talk to! A little child!... But you're no fool, Stevy. See here now, an' remember. You know what's come to your father? He's killed, wilful; murdered, like what they hang people for, at Newgate, Stevy, by the law. An' do you know who's done it?"

I was distressed and bewildered, as well as alarmed by the old man's vehemence. "The captain," I said, whimpering again.

"Viney!" my grandfather shouted. "Henry Viney, as I might ha' served the same way, an' I wish I had! Viney and Marr's done it; an' Marr's paid for it already. Lord, Lord!" he went on, with his face down in his hands and his elbows on his knees. "Lord! I see a lot of it now! It was what they made out o' the insurance that was to save the firm; an' when my boy put in an' stopped it all the voyage out, an' more, they could hold on no longer, but plotted to get out with what they could lay hold of. Lord! it's plain as print, plain as print! Stevy!" He lowered his hands and looked up. "Stevy! that money's more yours now than ever. If I ever had a doubt—if it don't belong to the orphan they've made—but there, it's sent you, boy, sent you, an' any one 'ud believe in Providence after that."

In a moment more he was back at his earlier excitement. "But it's Viney's done it," he said, with his fist extended before him. "Remember, Stevy, when you grow up, it's Viney's done it, an' it's Murder, by the law of England. Viney has killed your father, an' if it was brought against him it 'ud be Murder!"

"Then," I said, "we'll go to the police station and they will catch him."

My grandfather's hand dropped. "Ah, Stevy, Stevy," he groaned, "you don't know, you don't know. It ain't enough for that, an' if it was—if it was, I can't; I can't—not with you to look after. I might do it, an' risk all, if it wasn't for that.... My God, it's a judgment on me—a cruel judgment! My own son—an' just the same way—just the same way!... I can't, Stevy, not with you to take care of. Stevy, I must keep myself safe for your sake, an' I can't raise a hand to punish Viney. I can't, Stevy, I can't; for I'm a guilty man myself, by the law of England—an' Viney knows it! Viney knows it! Though it wasn't wilful, as God's my judge!"

Grandfather Nat ended with a groan, and sat still, with his head bowed in his hands. Again I remembered, and now with something of awe, my innocent question: "Did you ever kill a man, Grandfather Nat?"

Still he sat motionless and silent, till I could endure it no longer: for in some way I felt frightened. So I went timidly and put my arm about his neck. I fancied, though I was not sure, that I could feel a tremble from his shoulders; but he was silent still. Nevertheless I was oddly comforted by the contact, and presently, like a dog anxious for notice, ventured to stroke the grey hair.

Soon then he dropped his hands and spoke. "I shouldn't ha' said it, Stevy; but I'm all shook an' worried, an' I talked wild. It was no need to say it, but there ain't a soul alive to speak to else, an' somehow I talk as it might be half to myself. But you know what about things I say—private things—don't you? Remember?" He sat erect again, and raised a forefinger warningly, even sternly. "Remember, Stevy!... But come—there's things to do. Give me the

81

letter. We'll get together any little things to be kep', papers an' what not, an' take 'em home. An' I'll have to think about the rest, what's best to be done; sell 'em, or what. But I dunno, I dunno!"

CHAPTER XVII
IN BLUE GATE

In her den at the black stair-top in Blue Gate, Musky Mag lurked, furtive and trembling, after the inquests at the Hole in the Wall. Where Dan Ogle might be hiding she could not guess, and she was torn between a hundred fears and perplexities. Dan had been seen, and could be identified; of that she was convinced, and more than convinced, since she had heard Mr. Cripps's testimony. Moreover she well remembered at what point in her own evidence the police-inspector had handed the note to the coroner, and she was not too stupid to guess the meaning of that. How could she warn Dan, how help or screen him, how put to act that simple fidelity that was the sole virtue remaining in her, all the greater for the loss of the rest? She had no money; on the other hand she was confident that Dan must have with him the whole pocket-book full of notes which had cost two lives already, and now seemed like to cost the life she would so gladly buy with her own; for they had not been found on Kipps's body, nor in any way spoken of at the inquest. But then he might fear to change them. He could scarcely carry a single one to the receivers who knew him, for his haunts would be watched; more, a reward was offered, and no receiver would be above making an extra fifty pounds on the transaction. For to her tortured mind it seemed every moment more certain that the cry was up, and not the police alone, but everybody else was on the watch to give the gallows its due. She was uneasy at having no message. Doubtless he needed her help, as he had needed it so often before; doubtless he would come for it if he could, but that would be to put his head in the noose. How could she reach him, and give it? Even if she had known where he lay, to go to him would be to lead the police after her, for she had no doubt that her own movements would be watched. She knew that the boat wherein he had escaped had been found on the opposite side of the river, and she, like others, judged from that that he might be lurking in some of the waterside rookeries of the south bank; the more as it was the commonest device of those "wanted" in Ratcliff or Wapping to "go for a change" to Rotherhithe or Bankside, and for those in a like predicament on the southern shores to come north in the same way. But again, to go in search of him were but to share with the police whatever luck might attend the quest. So that Musky Mag feared alike to stay at home and to go abroad; longed to find Dan, and feared it as much; wished to aid him, yet equally dreaded that he should come to her or that she should go to him. And there was nothing to do, therefore, but to wait and listen anxiously; to listen for voices, or footsteps, even for creaks on the stairs; for a whistle without that might be a signal; for an uproar or a sudden hush that might announce the coming of the police into Blue Gate; even for a whisper or a scratching at door or window wherewith the fugitive might approach, fearful lest the police were there before him. But at evening, when the place grew dark, and the thickest of the gloom drew together, to make a monstrous shadow on the floor, where once she had fallen over something in the dark—then she went and sat on the stair-head, watching and dozing and waking in terror.

So went a day and a night, and another day. The corners of the room grew dusk again, and with the afternoon's late light the table flung its shadow on that same place on the floor; so that she went and moved it toward the wall.

As she set it down she started and crouched, for now at last there was a step on the stair—an unfamiliar step. A woman's, it would seem, and stealthy. Musky Mag held by the table, and waited.

The steps ceased at the landing, and there was a pause. Then, with no warning knock, the door was pushed open, and a head was thrust in, covered by an old plaid shawl; a glance about the room, and the rest of the figure followed, closing the door behind it; and, the shawl being flung back from over the bonnet, there stood Mrs. Grimes, rusty and bony, slack-faced and sour.

Mrs. Grimes screwed her red nose at the woman before her, jerked up her crushed bonnet, and plucked her rusty skirt across her knees with the proper virtuous twitch. Then said Mrs. Grimes: "Where's my brother Dan?"

For a moment Musky Mag disbelieved eyes and ears together. The visit itself, even more than the question, amazed and bewildered her. She had been prepared for any visitor but this. For Mrs. Grimes's relationship to Dan Ogle was a thing that exemplary lady made as close a secret as she could, as in truth was very natural. She valued herself on her respectability; she was the widow of a decent lighterman, of a decent lightering and wharf-working

83

family, and she called herself "house-keeper" (though she might be scarce more than charwoman) at the Hole in the Wall. She had never acknowledged her lawless brother when she could in any way avoid it, and she had, indeed, bargained that he should not come near her place of employment, lest he compromise her; and so far from seeking him out in his lodgings, she even had a way of failing to see him in the street. What should she want in Blue Gate at such a time as this, asking thus urgently for her brother Dan? What but the reward? For an instant Mag's fears revived with a jump, though even as it came she put away the fancy that such might be the design of any sister, however respectable.

"Where's my brother Dan?" repeated Mrs. Grimes, abruptly.

"I—I don't know, mum," faltered Mag, husky and dull. "I ain't seen 'im for—for—some time."

"O, nonsense. I want 'im particular. I got somethink to tell 'im important. If you won't say where 'e is, go an' find 'im."

"I wish I could, mum, truly. But I can't."

"Do you mean 'e's left you?" Mrs. Grimes bridled high, and helped it with a haughty sniff.

"No, mum, not quite, in your way of speakin', I think, mum. But 'e's—'e's just gone away for a bit."

"Ho. In trouble again, you mean, eh?"

"O, no, mum, not there," Mag answered readily; for, with her, "trouble" was merely a genteel name for gaol. "Not there—not for a long while."

"Where then?"

"That's what I dunno, mum; not at all."

Mrs. Grimes tightened her lips and glared; plainly she believed none of these denials. "P'raps 'e's wanted," she snapped, "an' keepin' out o' the way just now. Is that it?"

This was what no torture would have made Mag acknowledge; but, with all her vehemence of denial, her discomposure was plain to see. "No, mum, not that," she declared, pleadingly. "Reely 'e ain't, mum—reely 'e ain't; not that!"

"Pooh!" exclaimed Mrs. Grimes, seating herself with a flop. "That's a lie, plain enough. 'E's layin' up somewhere, an' you know it. What harm d'ye suppose I'm goin' to do 'im? 'E ain't robbed me— leastways not lately. I got a job for 'im, I tell you—money in 'is pocket. If you won't tell me, go an' tell 'im; go on. An' I'll wait."

"It's Gawd's truth, mum, I don't know where 'e is," Mag protested earnestly. "'Ark! there's someone on the stairs! They'll 'ear. Go away, mum, do. I'll try an' find 'im an' tell 'im—s'elp me I will! Go away—they're comin'!"

84

In truth the footsteps had reached the stair-top, and now, with a thump, the door was thrust open, and Blind George appeared, his fiddle under his arm, his stick sweeping before him, and his white eye rolling at the ceiling.

"Hullo!" he sung out. "Lady visitors! Or is it on'y one? 'Tain't polite to tell the lady to go away, Mag! Good afternoon, mum, good afternoon!" He nodded and grinned at upper vacancy, as one might at a descending angel; Mrs. Grimes, meanwhile, close at his elbow, preparing to get away as soon as he was clear past her. For Blind George's keenness of hearing was well known, and she had no mind he should guess her identity.

"Good afternoon, mum!" the blind man repeated. "Havin' tea?" He advanced another step, and extended his stick. "What!" he added, suddenly turning. "What! Table gone? What's this? Doin' a guy? Clearin' out?"

"No, George," Mag answered. "I only moved the table over to the wall. 'Ere it is—come an' feel it." She made a quick gesture over his shoulder, and Mrs. Grimes hurried out on tip-toe.

But at the first movement Blind George turned sharply. "There she goes," he said, making for the door. "She don't like me. Timid little darlin'! Hullo, my dear!" he roared down the stairs. "Hullo! you never give me a kiss! I know you! Won't you say good-bye?"

He waited a moment, listening intently; but Mrs. Grimes scuttled into the passage below without a word, and instantly Blind George supplemented his endearments with a burst of foul abuse, and listened again. This expedient succeeded no better than the first, and Mrs. Grimes was gone without a sound that might betray her identity.

Blind George shut the door. "Who was that?" he asked.

"Oh, nobody partic'lar," Mag answered with an assumption of indifference. "On'y a woman I know—name o' Jane. What d'you want?"

"Ah, now you're come to it." Blind George put his fiddle and bow on the table and groped for a chair. "Fust," he went on, "is there anybody else as can 'ear? Eh? Cracks or crannies or peepholes, eh? 'Cause I come as a pal, to talk private business, I do."

"It's all right, George; nobody can hear. What is it?"

"Why," said the blind man, catching her tight by the arm, and leaning forward to whisper; "it's Dan, that's what it is. It's Dan!"

She was conscious of a catching of the breath and a thump of the heart; and Blind George knew it too, for he felt it through the arm.

"It's Dan," he repeated. "So now you know if it's what you'd like listened to."

"Go on," she said.

"Ah. Well, fust thing, all bein' snug, 'ere's five bob; catch 'old." He slid his right hand down to her wrist, and with his left pressed the money into hers. "All right, don't be frightened of it, it won't 'urt ye! Lord, I bet Dan 'ud do the same for me if I wanted it, though 'e is a bit rough sometimes. I ain't rich, but I got a few bob by me; an' if a pal ain't to 'ave 'em, who is? Eh? Who is?"

He grinned under the white eye so ghastly a counterfeit of friendly good-will that the woman shrank, and pulled at the wrist he held.

"Lord love ye," he went on, holding tight to the wrist, "I ain't the bloke to round on a pal as is under a cloud. See what I might 'a' done, if I'd 'a' wanted. I might 'a' gone an' let out all sorts o' things, as you know very well yerself, at the inquest—both the inquests. But did I? Not me. Not a bit of it. That ain't my way. No; I lay low, an' said nothing. What arter that? Why, there's fifty quid reward offered, fifty quid—a fortune to a pore bloke like me. An' all I got to do is to go and say 'Dan Ogle' to earn it—them two words an' no more. Ain't that the truth? D'y' hear, ain't that the truth?"

He tugged at her wrist to extort an answer, and the woman's face was drawn with fear. But she made a shift to say, with elaborate carelessness, "Reward? What reward, George? I dunno nothin' about it."

"Gr-r-r!" he growled, pushing the wrist back, but gripping it still. "That ain't 'andsome, not to a pal it ain't; not to a faithful pal as comes to do y' a good turn. You know all about it well enough; an' you needn't think as I don't know too. Blind, ain't I? Blind from a kid, but not a fool! You ought to know that by this time—not a fool. Look 'ere!"—with another jerk at the woman's arm—"look 'ere. The last time I was in this 'ere room there was me an' you an' Dan an' two men as is dead now, an' post-mortalled, an' inquested an' buried, wasn't there? Well, Dan chucked me out. I ain't bearin' no malice for that, mind ye—ain't I just give ye five bob, an' ain't I come to do ye a turn? I was chucked out, but ye don't s'pose I dunno what 'appened arter I was gone, do ye? Eh?"

The room was grown darker, and though the table was moved, the shadow on the floor took its old place, and took its old shape, and grew; but it was no more abhorrent than the shadowy face with its sightless white eye close before hers, and the hand that held her wrist, and by it seemed to feel the pulse of her very mind. She struggled to her feet.

"Let go my wrist," she said. "I'll light a candle. You can go on."

"Don't light no candle on my account," he said, chuckling, as he let her hand drop. "It's a thing I never treat myself to. There's parties as is afraid o' the dark, they tell me—I'm used to it."

She lit the candle, and set it where it lighted best the place of the shadow. Then she returned and stood by the chair she had been sitting in. "Go on," she said again. "What's this good turn you want to do me?"

"Ah," he replied, "that's the pint!" He caught her wrist again with a sudden snatch, and drew her forward. "Sit down, my gal, sit down, an' I'll tell ye comfortable. What was I a-sayin'? Oh, what 'appened arter I was gone; yes. Well, that there visitor was flimped clean, clean as a whistle; but fust—eh?—fust!" Blind George snapped his jaws, and made a quick blow in the air with his stick. "Eh? Eh? Ah, well, never mind! But now I'll tell you what the job fetched. Eight 'undred an' odd quid in a leather pocket-book, an' a silver watch! Eh? I thought that 'ud make ye jump. Blind, ain't I? Blind from a kid,—but not a fool!"

"Well now," he proceeded, "so far all right. If I can tell ye that, I can pretty well tell ye all the rest, can't I? All about Bob Kipps goin' off to sell the notes, an' Dan watchin' 'im, bein' suspicious, an' catchin' 'im makin' a bolt for the river, an'—eh?" He raised the stick in his left hand again, but now point forward, with a little stab toward her breast. "Eh? Eh? Like that, eh? All right—don't be frightened. I'm a pal, I am. It served that cove right, I say, playin' a trick on a pal. I don't play a trick on a pal. I come 'ere to do 'im a good turn, I do. Don't I?—Well, Dan got away, an' good luck to 'im. 'E got away, clear over the river, with the eight 'undred quid in the leather pocket-book. An' now 'e's a-layin' low an' snug, an' more good luck to 'im, says I, bein' a pal. Ain't that right?"

Mag shuffled uneasily. "Go on," she said, "if you think you know such a lot. You ain't come to that good turn yet that you talk so much about."

"Right! Now I'll come to it. Now you know I know as much as anybody—more'n anybody 'cept Dan, p'rhaps a bit more'n what you know yourself; an' I kep' it quiet when I might 'a' made my fortune out of it; kep' it quiet, bein' a faithful pal. An' bein' a faithful pal an' all I come 'ere with five bob for ye, bein' all I can afford, 'cos I know you're a bit short, though Dan's got plenty—got a fortune. Why should you be short, an' Dan got a fortune? On'y 'cos you want a pal as you can trust, like me! That's all. 'E can't come to you 'cos o' showin' 'isself. You can't go to 'im 'cos of being watched an' follered. So I come to do ye both a good turn goin' between, one to another. Where is 'e?"

Mag was in some way reassured. She feared and distrusted Blind George, and she was confounded to learn how much he knew: but at least he was still ignorant of the essential thing. So she said, "Knowin' so much more'n me, I wonder you dunno that too. Any'ow I don't."

"What? You dunno. Dunno where 'e is?"

"No, I don't; no more'n you."

"O, that's all right—all right for anybody else; but not for a pal like me—not for a pal as is doin' y' a good turn. Besides, it ain't you on'y; it's 'im. 'Ow'll 'e get on with the stuff? 'E won't be able to change it, an' 'e'll be as short as you, an' p'rhaps get smugged with it on 'im. That 'ud never do; an' I can get it changed. What part o' Rotherhithe is it, eh? I can easy find 'im. Is it Dockhead?"

"There or anywhere, for all I know. I tell ye, George, I dunno no more'n you. Let go my arm, go on."

But he gave it another pull—an angry one. "What? What?" he cried. "If Dan knowed as you was keepin' 'is ol' pal George from doin' 'im a good turn, what 'ud 'e do, eh? 'E'd give it you, my beauty, wouldn't 'e? Eh? Eh?" He twisted the arm, ground his teeth, and raised his stick menacingly.

But this was a little too much. He was a man, and stronger, but at any rate he was blind. She rose and struggled to twist her arm from his grasp. "If you don't put down that stick, George," she said, "if you don't put it down an' let go my arm, I'll give it you same as Bob Kipps got it—s'elp me I will! I'll give you the chive—I will! Don't you make me desprit!"

He let go the wrist and laughed. "Whoa, beauty!" he cried; "don't make a rumpus with a faithful pal! If you won't tell me I s'pose you won't, bein' a woman; whether it's bad for Dan or not, eh?"

"I tell you I can't, George; I swear solemn I dunno no more'n you—p'rhaps not so much. 'E ain't bin near nor sent nor nothing, since—since then. That's gospel truth. If I do 'ear from 'im I'll—well then I'll see."

"Will ye tell 'im, then? 'Ere, tell 'im this. Tell 'im he mustn't go tryin' to sell them notes, or 'e'll be smugged. Tell 'im I can put 'im in the way o' gettin' money for 'em—'ard quids, an' plenty on 'em. Tell 'im that, will ye? Tell 'im I'm a faithful pal, an' nobody can do it but me. I know things you don't know about, nor 'im neither. Tell 'im to-night. Will ye tell 'im to-night?"

"'Ow can I tell 'im to-night? I'll tell 'im right enough when I see 'im. I s'pose you want to make your bit out of it, pal or not."

"There y'are!" he answered quickly. "There y'are! If you won't believe in a pal, look at that! If I make a fair deal, man to man, with them notes, an' get money for 'em instead o' smuggin'—quids instead o' quod—I'll 'ave my proper reg'lars, won't I? An' proper reg'lars on all that, paid square, 'ud be more'n I could make playin' the snitch, if Dan'll be open to reason. See? You won't forget, eh?" He took her arm again eagerly, above the elbow. "Know what to say, don't ye? Best for all of us. 'E mustn't show them notes to a soul, till 'e sees me. I'm a pal. I got the little tip 'ow to do it proper—see? Now you know. Gimme my fiddle. 'Ere we are. Where's the door? All right—don't forget!"

Blind George clumped down the black stair, and so reached the street of Blue Gate. At the door he paused, listening till he was satisfied of Musky Mag's movements above; then he walked a few yards along the dark street, and stopped.

From a black archway across the street a man came skulking out, and over the roadway to Blind George's side. It was Viney. "Well?" he asked eagerly. "What's your luck?"

Blind George swore vehemently, but quietly. "Precious little," he answered. "She dunno where 'e is. I thought at first it was kid, but it ain't. She ain't 'eard, an' she dunno. I couldn't catch hold o' the other woman, an' she got away an' never spoke. You see 'er again when she came out, didn't ye? Know 'er?"

"Not me—she kept her shawl tighter about her head than ever. An' if she hadn't it ain't likely I'd know her. What now? Stand watch again? I'm sick of it."

"So am I, but it's for good pay, if it comes off. Five minutes might do it. You get back, an' wait in case I tip the whistle."

Viney crept growling back to his arch, and Blind George went and listened at Mag's front door for a few moments more. Then he turned into the one next it, and there waited, invisible, listening still.

Five minutes went, and did not do it, and ten minutes went, and five times ten. Blue Gate lay darkling in evening, and foul shadows moved about it. From one den and another came a drawl and a yaup of drunken singing; a fog from the river dulled the lights at the Highway end, and slowly crept up the narrow way. It was near an hour since Viney and Blind George had parted, when there grew visible, coming through the mist from the Highway, the uncertain figure of a stranger: drifting dubiously from door to door, staring in

89

at one after another, and wandering out toward the gutter to peer ahead in the gloom.

Blind George could hear, as well as another could see, that here was a stranger in doubt, seeking somebody or some house. Soon the man, middle-sized, elderly, a trifle bent, and all dusty with lime, came in turn to the door where he stood; and at once Blind George stepped full against him with an exclamation and many excuses.

"Beg pardon, guv'nor! Pore blind chap! 'Ope I didn't 'urt ye! Was ye wantin' anybody in this 'ouse?"

The limy man looked ahead, and reckoned the few remaining doors to the end of Blue Gate. "Well," he said, "I fancy it's 'ere or next door. D'ye know a woman o' the name o' Mag—Mag Flynn?"

"I'm your bloke, guv'nor. Know 'er? Rather. Up 'ere—I'll show ye. Lord love ye, she's an old friend o' mine. Come on.... I should say you'd be in the lime trade, guv'nor, wouldn't you? I smelt it pretty strong, an' I'll never forget the smell o' lime. Why, says you? Why, 'cos o' losin' my blessed sight with lime, when I was a innocent kid. Fell on a slakin'—bed, guv'nor, an' blinded me blessed self; so I won't forget the smell o' lime easy. Ain't you in the trade, now? Ain't I right?" He stopped midway on the stairs to repeat the question. "Ain't I right? Is it yer own business or a firm?"

"Ah well, I do 'ave to do with lime a good bit," said the stranger, evasively. "But go on, or else let me come past."

Blind George turned, and reaching the landing, thumped his stick on the door and pushed it open. "'Ere y'are," he sang out. "'Ere's a genelman come to see ye, as I found an' showed the way to. Lord love ye, 'e'd never 'a' found ye if it wasn't for me. But I'm a old pal, ain't I? A faithful old pal!"

He swung his stick till he found a chair, and straightway sat in it, like an invited guest. "Lord love ye, yes," he continued, rolling his eye and putting his fiddle across his knees; "one o' the oldest pals she's got, or 'im either."

The newcomer looked in a puzzled way from Blind George to the woman, and back again. "It's private business I come about," he said, shortly.

"All right, guv'nor," shouted Blind George, heartily, "Out with it! We're all pals 'ere! Old pals!"

"You ain't my old pal, anyhow," the limy man observed. "An' if the room's yours, we'll go an' talk somewheres else."

"Get out, George, go along," said Mag, with some asperity, but more anxiety. "You clear out, go on."

"O, all right, if you're goin' to be unsociable," said the fiddler, rising. "Damme, I don't want to stay—not me. I was on'y doin' the friendly, that's all; bein' a old pal. But I'm off all right—I'm off. So long!"

He hugged his fiddle once more, and clumped down into the street. He tapped with his stick till he struck the curb, and then crossed the muddy roadway; while Viney emerged again from the dark arch to meet him.

"All right," said Blind George, whispering huskily. "It's business now, I think—business. You come on now. You'll 'ave to foller 'em if they come out together. If they don't—well, you must look arter the one as does."

CHAPTER XVIII
ON THE COP

When the limy man left Blue Gate he went, first, to the Hole in the Wall, there to make to Captain Kemp some small report on the wharf by the Lea. This did not keep him long, and soon he was on his journey home to the wharf itself, by way of the crooked lanes and the Commercial Road.

He had left Blue Gate an hour and more when Musky Mag emerged from her black stairway, peering fearfully about the street ere she ventured her foot over the step. So she stood for a few seconds, and then, as one chancing a great risk, stepped boldly on the pavement, and, turning her back to the Highway, walked toward Back Lane. This was the nearer end of Blue Gate, and, the corner turned, she stopped short, and peeped back. Satisfied that she had no follower, she crossed Back Lane, and taking every corner, as she came to it, with a like precaution, threaded the maze of small, ill-lighted streets that lay in the angle between the great Rope Walk and Commercial Road. This wide road she crossed, and then entered the dark streets beyond, in rear of the George Tavern; and so, keeping to obscure parallel ways, sometimes emerging into the glare of the main road, more commonly slinking in its darker purlieus, but never out of touch with it, she travelled east; following in the main the later course of the limy man, who had left Blue Gate by its opposite end.

The fog, that had dulled the lights in Ratcliff Highway, met

91

her again near Limehouse Basin; but, ere she reached the church, she was clear of it once more. Beyond, the shops grew few, and the lights fewer. For a little while decent houses lined the way: the houses of those last merchants who had no shame to live near the docks and the works that brought their money. At last, amid a cluster of taverns and shops that were all for the sea and them that lived on it, the East India Dock gates stood dim and tall, flanked by vast raking walls, so that one might suppose a Chinese city to seethe within. And away to the left, the dark road that the wall overshadowed was lined on the other side by hedge and ditch, with meadows and fields beyond, that were now no more than a vast murky gulf; so that no stranger peering over the hedge could have guessed aright if he looked on land or on water, or on mere black vacancy.

Here the woman made a last twist: turning down a side street, and coming to a moment's stand in an archway. This done, she passed through the arch into a path before a row of ill-kept cottages; and so gained the marshy field behind the Accident Hospital, the beginning of the waste called The Cop.

Here the great blackness was before her and about her, and she stumbled and laboured on the invisible ground, groping for pits and ditches, and standing breathless again and again to listen. The way was so hard as to seem longer than it was, and in the darkness she must needs surmount obstacles that in daylight she would have turned. Often a ditch barred her way; and when, after long search, a means of crossing was found, it was commonly a plank to be traversed on hands and knees. There were stagnant pools, too, into which she walked more than once; and twice she suffered a greater shock of terror: first at a scurry of rats, and later at quick footsteps following in the sodden turf—the footsteps, after all, of nothing more terrible than a horse of inquiring disposition, out at grass.

So she went for what seemed miles: though there was little more than half a mile in a line from where she had left the lights to where at last she came upon a rough road, seamed with deep ruts, and made visible by many whitish blotches where lime had fallen, and had there been ground into the surface. To the left this road stretched away toward the lights of Bromley and Bow Common, and to the right it rose by an easy slope over the river wall skirting the Lea, and there ended at Kemp's Wharf.

Not a creature was on the road, and no sound came from the black space behind her. With a breath of relief she set foot on the firmer ground, and hurried up the slope. From the top of the bank she could see Kemp's Wharf just below, with two dusty lighters

92

moored in the dull river; and beyond the river the measureless, dim Abbey Marsh. Nearer, among the sheds, a dog barked angrily at the sound of strange feet.

A bright light came from the window of the little house that made office and dwelling for the wharf-keeper, and something less of the same light from the open door; for there the limy man stood waiting, leaning on the door-post, and smoking his pipe.

He grunted a greeting as Mag came down the bank. "Bit late," he said. "But it ain't easy over the Cop for a stranger."

"Where?" the woman whispered eagerly. "Where is he?"

The limy man took three silent pulls at his pipe. Then he took it from his mouth with some deliberation, and said: "Remember what I said? I don't want 'im 'ere. I dunno what 'e's done, an' don't want; but if 'e likes to come 'idin' about, I ain't goin' to play the informer. I dunno why I should promise as much as that, just 'cos my brother married 'is sister. She ain't done me no credit, from what I 'ear now. Though she 'ad a good master, as I can swear; 'cos 'e's mine too."

"Where is he?" was all Mag's answer, again in an anxious whisper.

"Unnerstand?" the limy man went on. "I'm about done with the pair on 'em now, but I ain't goin' to inform. 'E come 'ere a day or two back an' claimed shelter; an' seein' as I was goin' up to Wappin' to-night, 'e wanted me to tell you where 'e was. Well, I've done that, an' I ain't goin' to do no more; see? 'E ain't none o' mine, an' I won't 'ave part nor parcel with 'im, nor any of ye. I keep myself decent, I do. I shan't say 'e's 'ere an' I shan't say 'e ain't; an' the sooner 'e goes the better 'e'll please me. See?"

"Yes, Mr. Grimes, sir; but tell me where he is!"

The limy man took his pipe from his mouth, and pointed with a comprehensive sweep of the stem at the sheds round about. "You can go an' look in any o' them places as ain't locked," he said off-handedly. "The dog's chained up. Try the end one fust."

Grimes the wharfinger resumed his pipe, and Mag scuffled off to where the light from the window fell on the white angle of a small wooden shelter. The place was dark within, dusted about with lime, and its door stood inward. She stopped and peered.

"All right," growled Dan Ogle from the midst of the dark. "Can't ye see me now y' 'ave come?" And he thrust his thin face and big shoulders out through the opening.

"O Dan!" the woman cried, putting out her hands as though she would take him by the neck, but feared repulse. "O Dan! Thank Gawd you're safe, Dan! I bin dyin' o' fear for you, Dan!"

"G-r-r-r!" he snorted. "Stow that! What I want's money. Got any?"

CHAPTER XIX
ON THE COP

It was at a bend of the river-wall by the Lea, in sight of Kemp's Wharf, that Dan Ogle and his sister met at last. Dan had about as much regard for her as she had for him, and the total made something a long way short of affection. But common interests brought them together. Mrs. Grimes had told Mag that she knew of something that would put money in Dan's pocket; and, as money was just what Dan wanted in his pocket, he was ready to hear what his sister had to tell: more especially as it seemed plain that she was unaware—exactly—of the difficulty that had sent him into hiding.

So, instructed by Mag, she came to the Cop on a windy morning, where, from the top of the river-wall, one might look east over the Abbey Marsh, and see an unresting and unceasing press of grey and mottled cloud hurrying up from the flat horizon to pass overhead, and vanish in the smoke of London to the West. Mrs. Grimes avoided the wharf; for she saw no reason why her brother-in-law, her late employer's faithful servant, should witness her errand. She climbed the river-wall at a place where it neared the road at its Bromley end, and thence she walked along the bank-top.

Arrived where it made a sharp bend, she descended a little way on the side next the river, and there waited. Dan, on the look-out from his shed, spied her be-ribboned bonnet from afar, and went quietly and hastily under shelter of the river-wall toward where she stood. Coming below her on the tow-path, he climbed the bank, and brother and sister stood face to face; unashamed ruffianism looking shabby respectability in the eyes.

"Umph," growled Dan. "So 'ere y'are, my lady."

"Yes," the woman answered, "'ere I am; an' there you are—a nice respectable sort of party for a brother!"

"Ah, ain't I? If I was as respectable as my sister I might get a job up at the Hole in the Wall, mightn't I? 'Specially as I 'ear as there's a vacancy through somebody gettin' the sack over a cash-box!"

Mrs. Grimes glared and snapped. "I s'pose you got that from

'im," she said, jerking her head in the direction of the wharf. "Well, I ain't come 'ere to call names—I come about that same cash-box; at any rate I come about what's in it.... Dan, there's a pile o' bank notes in that box, that don't belong to Cap'en Nat Kemp no more'n they belong to you or me! Nor as much, p'raps, if you'll put up a good way o' gettin' at 'em!"

"You put up a way as wasn't a good un, seemin'ly," said Dan. "'Ow d'ye mean they don't belong to Kemp?"

"There was a murder at the Hole in the Wall; a week ago."

"Eh?" Dan's jaw shut with a snap, and his eye was full of sharp inquiry.

"A man was stabbed against the bar-parlour door, an' the one as did it got away over the river. One o' the two dropped a leather pocket-book full o' notes, an' the kid—Kemp's grandson—picked it up in the rush when nobody see it. I see it, though, afterward, when the row was over. I peeped from the stairs, an' I see Kemp open it an' take out notes—bunches of 'em—dozens!"

"Ah, you did, did ye?" Dan observed, staring hard at his sister. "Bunches o' bank notes—dozens. See a photo, too? Likeness of a woman an' a boy? 'Cos it was there."

Mrs. Grimes stared now. "Why, yes," she said. "But—but 'ow do you come to know? Eh?... Dan!... Was you—was you——"

"Never mind whether I was nor where I was. If it 'adn't been for you I'd a had them notes now, safe an' snug, 'stead o' Cap'en Nat. You lost me them!"

"I did?"

"Yes, you. Wouldn't 'ave me come to the Hole in the Wall in case Cap'en Nat might guess I was yer brother—bein' so much like ye! Like you! G-r-r-r! 'Ope I ain't got a face like that!"

"Ho yes! You're a beauty, Dan Ogle, ain't ye? But what's all that to do with the notes?" Mrs. Grimes's face was blank with wonder and doubt, but in her eyes there was a growing and hardening suspicion. "What's all that to do with the notes?"

"It's all to do with 'em. 'Cos o' that I let another chap bring a watch to sell, 'stead o' takin' it myself. An' 'e come back with a fine tale about Cap'en Nat offerin' to pay 'igh for them notes; an' so I was fool enough to let 'im take them too, 'stead o' goin' myself. But I watched 'im, though—watched 'im close. 'E tried to make a bolt—an'—an' so Cap'en Nat got the notes after all, it seems, then?"

"Dan," said Mrs. Grimes retreating a step; "Dan, it was you! It was you, an' you're hiding for it!"

The man stood awkward and sulky, like a loutish schoolboy, detected and defiant.

"Well," he said at length, "s'pose it was? You ain't got no proof of it; an' if you 'ad——What 'a' ye come 'ere for, eh?"

She regarded him now with a gaze of odd curiosity, which lasted through the rest of their talk; much as though she were convinced of some extraordinary change in his appearance, which nevertheless eluded her observation.

"I told you what I come for," she answered, after a pause. "About gettin' them notes away from Kemp—the old wretch!"

"Umph! Old wretch. 'Cos 'e wanted to keep 'is cash-box, eh? Well, what's the game?"

Mrs. Grimes in no way abated her intent gaze, but she came a little closer, with a sidling step, as if turning her back to a possible listener. "There was two inquests at the Hole in the Wall," she said; "two on the same day. There was Kipps, as lost the notes when Cap'en Kemp got 'em. An' there was Marr the shipowner—an' it was 'im as lost 'em first!"

She took a pace back as she said this, looking for its effect. But Dan made no answer. Albeit his frown grew deeper and his eye sharper, and he stood alert, ready to treat his sister as friend or enemy according as she might approve herself.

"Marr lost 'em first," she repeated, "an' I can very well guess how, though when I came here I didn't know you was in it. How did I know, thinks you, that Marr lost 'em first? I got eyes, an' I got ears, an' I got common sense; an' I see the photo you spoke of—Marr an' 'is mother, most likely; anyhow the boy was Marr, plain, whoever the woman was. It on'y wanted a bit o' thinkin' to judge what them notes had gone through. But I didn't dream you was so deep in it! Lor, no wonder Mag was frightened when I see 'er!"

Still Dan said nothing, but his eyes seemed brighter and smaller—perhaps dangerous.

So the woman proceeded quickly: "It's all right! You needn't be frightened of my knowin' things! All the more reason for your gettin' the notes now, if you lost 'em before. But it's halves for me, mind ye. Ain't it halves for me?"

Dan was silent for a moment. Then he growled, "We ain't got 'em yet."

"No, but it's halves when we do get 'em; or else I won't say another word. Ain't it halves?"

Dan Ogle could afford any number of promises, if they would win him information. "All right," he said. "Halves it is, then, when we get 'em. An' how are we goin' to do it?"

Mrs. Grimes sidled closer again. "Marr the shipowner lost 'em first," she said, "an' he was pulled out o' the river, dead an' murdered, just at the back o' the Hole in the Wall. See?"

"Well?"

"Don't see it? Kemp's got the pocket-book."

"Yes."

"Don't see it yet? Well; there's more. There's a room at the back o' the Hole in the Wall, where it stands on piles, with a trap-door over the water. The police don't know there's a trap-door there. I do."

Dan Ogle was puzzled and suspicious. "What's the good o' that?" he asked.

"I didn't think you such a fool, Dan Ogle. There's a man murdered with notes on him, an' a photo, an' a watch—you said there was a watch. He's found in the river just behind the Hole in the Wall. There's a trap-door—secret—at the Hole in the Wall, over the water; just the place he might 'a' been dropped down after he was killed. An' Kemp the landlord's got the notes an' the pocket-book an' the photo all complete; an' most likely the watch too, since you tell me he bought it; an' Viney could swear to 'em. Ain't all that enough to hang Cap'en Nat Kemp, if the police was to drop in sudden on the whole thing?"

Dan's mouth opened, and his face cleared a little. "I s'pose," he said, "you mean you might put it on to the police as it was Cap'en Nat did it; an' when they searched they'd find all the stuff, an' the pocket-book, an' the watch, an' the likeness, an' the trap-door; an' that 'ud be evidence enough to put 'im on the string?"

"Of course I mean it," replied Mrs. Grimes, with hungry spite in her eyes. "Of course I mean it! An' dearly I'd love to see it done, too! Cap'en Nat Kemp, with 'is money an' 'is gran'son 'e's goin' to make a gentleman of, an' all! "Ope you'll be honest where you go next,' says Cap'en Kemp, 'whether you're grateful to me or not!' Honest an' grateful! I'll give 'im honest an' grateful!"

Dan Ogle grinned silently. "No," he said, "you won't forgive 'im, I bet, if it was only 'cos you began by makin' such a pitch to marry 'im!" A chuckle broke from behind the grin. "You'd rather hang him than get his cash-box now, I'll swear!"

Mrs. Grimes was red with anger. "I would that!" she cried. "You're nearer truth than you think, Dan Ogle! An' if you say too much you'll lose the money you're after, for I'll go an' do it! So now!"

Dan clicked his tongue derisively. "Thought you'd come to tell me how to get the stuff," he said. "'Stead o' that you tell me how to hang Cap'en Nat, very clever, an' lose it. I don't see that helps us."

"Go an' threaten him."

"Threaten Cap'en Nat?" exclaimed Dan, glaring contempt, and spitting it. "Oh yes, I see myself! Cap'en Nat ain't that sort o' mug. I'm as 'ard as most, but I ain't 'ard enough for a job like that: or soft enough, for that's what I'd be to try it on. Lor' lumme! Go an' ask any man up the Highway to face Cap'en Nat, an' threaten him! Ask the biggest an' toughest of 'em. Ask Jim Crute, with his ear like a blue-bag, that he chucked out o' the bar like a kitten, last week! 'Cap'en Nat,' says I, 'if you don't gimme eight hundred quid, I'll hit you a crack!' Mighty fine plan that! That 'ud get it, wouldn't it? Ah, it 'ud get something!"

"I didn't say that sort of threat, you fool! You've got no sense for anything but bashing. There's the evidence that 'ud hang him; go an' tell him that, and say he shall swing for it, if he doesn't hand over!"

Dan stared long and thoughtfully. Then his lip curled again. "Pooh!" he said. "I'm a fool, am I? O! Anyhow, whether I am or not, I'm a fool's brother. Threaten Cap'en Nat with the evidence, says you! What evidence? The evidence what he's got in his own hands! S'pose I go, like a mug, an' do it. Fust thing he does, after he's kicked me out, is to chuck the pocket-book an' the likeness on the fire, an' the watch in the river. Then he changes the notes, or sells 'em abroad, an' how do we stand then? Why, you're a bigger fool than I thought you was!... What's that?"

It was nothing but a gun on the marsh, where a cockney sportsman was out after anything he could hit. But Dan Ogle's nerves were alert, and throughout the conversation he had not relaxed his watch toward London; so that the shot behind disturbed him enough to break the talk.

"We've been here long enough," he said. "You hook it. I'll see about Cap'en Nat. Your way's no good. I'll try another, an' if that don't come off—well, then you can hang him if you like, an' welcome. But now hook it, an' shut your mouth till I've had my go. 'Nough said. Don't go back the way you come."

CHAPTER XX

STEPHEN'S TALE

My father's death wrought in Grandfather Nat a change that awed me. He looked older and paler—even smaller. He talked less to me, but began, I fancied, to talk to himself. Withal, his manner was kinder than before, if that were possible; though it was with a sad kindness that distressed and troubled me. More than once I woke at night with candle-light on my face, and found him gazing down at me with a grave doubt in his eyes; whereupon he would say nothing, but pat my cheek, and turn away.

Early one evening as I sat in the bar-parlour, and my grandfather stood moodily at the door between that and the bar, a man came into the private compartment whom I had seen there frequently before. He was, in fact, the man who had brought the silver spoons on the morning when I first saw Ratcliff Highway, and he was perhaps the most regular visitor to the secluded corner of the bar. This time he slipped quietly and silently in at the door, and, remaining just within it, out of sight from the main bar, beckoned; his manner suggesting business above the common.

But my grandfather only frowned grimly, and stirred not as much as a finger. The man beckoned again, impatiently; but there was no favour in Grandfather Nat's eye, and he answered with a growl. At that the man grew more vehement, patted his breast pocket, jerked his thumb, and made dumb words with a great play of mouth.

"You get out!" said Grandfather Nat.

A shade of surprise crossed the man's face, and left plain alarm behind it. His eyes turned quickly toward the partition which hid the main bar from him, and he backed instantly to the door and vanished.

A little later the swing doors of the main bar were agitated, and an eye was visible between them, peeping. They parted, and disclosed the face of that same stealthy visitor but lately sent away from the other door. Reassured, as it seemed, by what he saw of the company present, he came boldly in, and called for a drink with an elaborate air of unconcern. But, as he took the glass from the potman, I could perceive a sidelong glance at my grandfather, and presently another. Captain Nat, however, disregarded him wholly; while the pale man, aware of he knew not what between them, looked alertly from one to the other, ready to abandon his long-established drink, or to remain by it, according to circumstances.

The man of the silver spoons looked indifferently from one occupant of the bar to the next, as he took his cold rum. There was the pale man, and Mr. Cripps, and a sailor, who had been pretty regular in the bar of late, and who, though noisy and apt to break into disjointed song, was not so much positively drunk as never wholly sober. And there were two others, regular frequenters both.

99

Having well satisfied himself of these, the man of the silver spoons finished his rum and walked out. Scarce had the door ceased to swing behind him, when he was once more in the private compartment, now with a knowing and secure smile, a cough and a nod. For plainly he supposed there must have been a suspicious customer in the house, who was now gone.

Grandfather Nat let fall the arm that rested against the door frame. "Out you go!" he roared. "If you want another drink the other bar's good enough for you. If you don't I don't want you here. So out you go!"

The man was dumbfounded. He opened his mouth as though to say something, but closed it again, and slunk backward.

"Out you go!" shouted the unsober sailor in the large bar. "Out you go! You 'bey orders, see? Lord, you'd better 'bey orders when it's Cap'en Kemp! Ah, I know, I do!" And he shook his head, stupidly sententious.

But the fellow was gone for good, and the pale man was all eyes, scratching his cheek feebly, and gazing on Grandfather Nat.

"Out he goes!" the noisy sailor went on. "That's cap'en's orders. Cap'en's orders or mate's orders, all's one. Like father, like son. Ah, I know!'"

"Ah," piped Mr. Cripps, "a marvellous fine orficer Cap'en Kemp must ha' been aboard ship, I'm sure. Might you ever ha' sailed under 'im?"

"Me?" cried the sailor with a dull stare. "Me? Under him?... Well no, not under him. But cap'en's orders or mate's orders, all's one."

"P'raps," pursued Mr. Cripps in a lower voice, with a glance over the bar, "p'raps you've been with young Mr. Kemp—the late?"

"Him?" This with another and a duller stare. "Him? Um! Ah, well—never mind. Never you mind, see? You mind your own business, my fine feller!"

Mr. Cripps retired within himself with no delay, and fixed an abstracted gaze in his half-empty glass. I think he was having a disappointing evening; people were disagreeable, and nobody had stood him a drink. More, Captain Nat had been quite impracticable of late, and for days all approaches to the subject of the sign, or the board to paint it on, had broken down hopelessly at the start. As to the man just sent away, Mr. Cripps seemed, and no doubt was, wholly indifferent. Captain Nat was merely exercising his authority in his own bar, as he did every day, and that was all.

But the pale man was clearly uneasy, and that with reason. For, as afterwards grew plain, the event was something greater than it seemed. Indeed, it was nothing less than the end of the indirect traffic in watches and silver spoons. From that moment every visitor to the private compartment was sent away with the same peremptory incivility; every one, save perhaps some rare stranger of the better sort, who came for nothing but a drink. So that, in course of a day or two, the private compartment went almost out of use; and the pale man's face grew paler and longer as the hours went. He came punctually every morning, as usual, and sat his time out with the stagnant drink before him, till he received my grandfather's customary order to "drink up"; and then vanished till the time appointed for his next attendance. But he made no more excursions into the side court after sellers of miscellaneous valuables. From what I know of my grandfather's character, I believe that the pale man must have been paid regular wages; for Grandfather Nat was not a man to cast off a faithful servant, though plainly the man feared it. At any rate there he remained with his perpetual drink; and so remained until many things came to an end together.

There was a certain relief, and, I think, an odd touch of triumph in Grandfather Nat's face and manner that night as he kissed me, and bade me good-night. As for myself, I did not realise the change, but I had a vague idea that my grandfather had sent away his customer on my account; and for long I lay awake, and wondered why.

CHAPTER XXI
IN THE BAR-PARLOUR

Stephen was sound asleep, and the Hole in the Wall had closed its eyes for the night. The pale man had shuffled off, with his doubts and apprehensions, toward the Highway, and Mr. Cripps was already home in Limehouse. Only the half-drunken sailor was within hail, groping toward some later tavern, and Captain Nat, as he extinguished the lamps in the bar, could hear his song in the distance—

The grub was bad an' the pay was low, Leave her, Johnny, leave her! So hump your duds an' ashore you go For it's time for us to leave her!

Captain Nat blew out the last light in the bar and went into the bar-parlour. He took out the cash-box, and stood staring thoughtfully at the lid for some seconds. He was turning at last to extinguish the lamp at his elbow, when there was a soft step without, and a cautious tap at the door.

Captain Nat's eyes widened, and the cash-box went back under the shelf. The tap was repeated ere the old man could reach the door and shoot back the bolts. This done, he took the lamp in his left hand, and opened the door.

In the black of the passage a man stood, tall and rough. Just such a figure Captain Nat had seen there before, less distinctly, and in a briefer glimpse; for indeed it was Dan Ogle.

"Well?" said Captain Nat.

"Good evenin', cap'en," Dan answered, with an uncouth mixture of respect and familiarity. "I jist want five minutes with you."

"O, you do, do you?" replied the landlord, reaching behind himself to set the lamp on the table. "What is it? I've a notion I've seen you before."

"Very like, cap'en. It's all right; on'y business."

"Then what's the business?"

Dan Ogle glanced to left and right in the gloom of the alley, and edged a step nearer. "Best spoke of indoors," he said, hoarsely. "Best for you an' me too. Nothin' to be afraid of—on'y business."

"Afraid of? Phoo! Come in, then."

Dan complied, with an awkward assumption of jaunty confidence, and Captain Nat closed the door behind him.

"Nobody to listen, I suppose?" asked Ogle.

"No, nobody. Out with it!"

"Well, cap'en, just now you thought you'd seen me before. Quite right; so you have. You see me in the same place—just outside that there door. An' I borrowed your boat."

"Umph!" Captain Nat's eyes were keen and hard. "Is your name Dan Ogle?"

"That's it, cap'en." The voice was confident, but the eye was shifty. "Now you know. A chap tried to do me, an' I put his light out. You went for me, an' chased me, but you stuck your hooks in the quids right enough." Dan Ogle tried a grin and a wink, but Captain Nat's frown never changed.

"Well, well," Dan went on, after a pause, "it's all right, anyhow. I outed the chap, an' you took care o' the ha'pence; so we helped each other, an' done it atween us. I just come along to-night to cut it up."

"Cut up what?"

"Why, the stuff. Eight hundred an' ten quid in notes, in a leather pocket-book. Though I ain't particular about the pocket-book." Dan tried another grin. "Four hundred an' five quid'll be good enough for me: though it ought to be more, seein' I got it first, an' the risk an' all."

Captain Nat, with a foot on a chair and a hand on the raised knee, relaxed not a shade of his fierce gaze. "Who told you," he asked presently, "that I had eight hundred an' ten pound in a leather pocket-book?"

"O, a little bird—just a pretty little bird, cap'en."

"Tell me the name o' that pretty little bird."

"Lord lumme, cap'en, don't be bad pals! It ain't a little bird what'll do any harm! It's all safe an' snug enough between us, an' I'm doin' it on the square, ain't I? I knowed about you, an' you didn't know about me; but I comes fair an' open, an' says it was me as done it, an' I on'y want a fair share up between pals in a job together. That's all right, ain't it?"

"Was it a pretty little bird in a bonnet an' a plaid shawl? A scraggy sort of a little bird with a red beak? The sort of little bird as likes to feather its nest with a cash-box—one as don't belong to it? Is that your pattern o' pretty little bird?"

"Well, well, s'pose it is, cap'en? Lord, don't be bad pals! I ain't, am I? Make things straight, an' I'll take care she don't go a pretty-birdin' about with the tale. I'll guarantee that, honourable. You ain't no need be afraid o' that."

"D'ye think I look afraid?"

"Love ye, cap'en, why, I didn't mean that! There ain't many what 'ud try to frighten you. That ain't my tack. You're too hard a nut for that, anybody knows." Dan Ogle fidgeted uneasily with a hand about his neck-cloth; while the other arm hung straight by his side. "But look here, now, cap'en," he went on; "you're a straight man, an' you don't round on a chap as trusts you. That's right ain't it?"

"Well?" Truly Captain Nat's piercing stare, his unwavering frown, were disconcerting. Dan Ogle had come confidently prepared to claim a share of the plunder, just as he would have done from any rascal in Blue Gate. But, in presence of the man he knew for his master, he had had to begin with no more assurance than he could force on himself; and now, though he had met not a word of refusal, he was reduced well-nigh to pleading. But he saw the best opening, as by a flash of inspiration; and beyond that he had another resource, if he could but find courage to use it.

"Well?" said Captain Nat.

"You're the sort as plays the square game with a man as trusts you, cap'en. Very well. I've trusted you. I come an' put myself in your way, an' told you free what I done, an' I ask, as man to man, for my fair whack o' the stuff. Bein' the straight man you are, you'll do the fair thing."

Captain Nat brought his foot down from the chair, and the knee from under his hand; and he clenched the hand on the table. But neither movement disturbed his steady gaze. So he stood for three seconds. Then, with an instant dart, he had Dan Ogle by the hanging arm, just above the wrist.

Dan sprang and struggled, but his wrist might have been chained to a post. Twice he made offer to strike at Captain Nat's face with the free hand, but twice the blow fainted ere it had well begun. Tall and powerful as he was, he knew himself no match for the old skipper. Pallid and staring, he whispered hoarsely: "No, cap'en—no! Drop it! Don't put me away! Don't crab the deal! D' y' 'ear——"

Captain Nat, grim and silent, slowly drew the imprisoned fore-arm forward, and plucked a bare knife from within the sleeve. There was blood on it, for his grip had squeezed arm and blade together.

"Umph!" growled Captain Nat; "I saw that in time, my lad"; and he stuck the knife in the shelf behind him.

"S'elp me, cap'en, I wasn't meanin' anythink—s'elp me I wasn't," the ruffian pleaded, cowering but vehement, with his neckerchief to his cut arm. "That's on'y where I carry it, s'elp me— on'y where I keep it!"

"Ah, I've seen it done before; but it's an awkward place if you get a squeeze," the skipper remarked drily. "Now you listen to me. You say you've come an' put yourself in my power, an' trusted me. So you have—with a knife up your sleeve. But never mind that—I doubt if you'd ha' had pluck to use it. You killed a man at my door, because of eight hundred pounds you'd got between you; but to get that money you had to kill another man first."

"No, cap'en, no——"

"Don't try to deny it, man! Why it's what's saving you! I know where that money come from—an' it's murder that got it. Marr was the man's name, an' he was a murderer himself; him an' another between 'em ha' murdered my boy; murdered him on the high seas as much as if it was pistol or poison. He was doin' his duty, an' it's murder, I tell you—murder, by the law of England! That man ought to ha' been hung, but he wasn't, an' he never would ha' been. He'd ha' gone free, except for you, an' made money of it. But you killed that man, Dan Ogle, an' you shall go free for it yourself; for that an' because I won't sell what you trusted me with about this other."

Captain Nat turned and took the knife from the shelf. "Now see," he went on. "You've done justice on a murderer, little as you meant it; but don't you come tryin' to take away the orphan's compensation—not as much as a penny of it! Don't you touch the compensation, or I'll give you up! I will that! Just you remember when you're safe. The man lied as spoke to seein' you that night by the door; an' now he's gone back on it, an' so you've nothing to fear from him, an' nothing to fear from the police. Nothing to fear from anybody but me; so you take care, Dan Ogle!... Come, enough said!"

Captain Nat flung wide the door and pitched the knife into the outer darkness. "There's your knife; go after it!"

CHAPTER XXII
ON THE COP

When Viney followed the limy man from Musky Mag's door he kept him well in view as far as the Hole in the Wall, and there waited. But when Grimes emerged, and Viney took up the chase, he had scarce made three-quarters of the way through the crooked lanes toward the Commercial Road, when, in the confusion and the darkness of the turnings, or in some stray rack of fog, the man of lime went wholly amissing. Viney hurried forward, doubled, and scoured the turnings about him. Drawing them blank, he hastened for the main road, and there consumed well nigh an hour in profitless questing to and fro; and was fain at last to seek out Blind George, and confess himself beaten.

But Blind George made a better guess. After Viney's departure in the wake of Grimes, he had stood patiently on guard in the black archway, and had got his reward. For he heard Musky Mag's feet descend her stairs; noted her timid pause at the door; and ear-watched her progress to the street corner. There she paused again, as he judged, to see that nobody followed; and then hurried out of earshot. He was no such fool as to attempt to dog a woman with eyes, but contented himself with the plain inference that she was on her way to see Dan Ogle, and that the man whom Viney was following had brought news of Dan's whereabouts; and with that he turned to the Highway and his fiddling. So that when he learned

105

that the limy man had called at the Hole in the Wall, and had gone out of Viney's sight on his way east, Blind George was quick to think of Kemp's Wharf, and to resolve that his next walk abroad should lead him to the Lea bank.

The upshot of this was that, after some trouble, Dan Ogle and Blind George met on the Cop, and that Dan consented to a business interview with Viney. He was confident enough in any dealings with either of them so long as he cockered in them the belief that he still had the notes. So he said very little, except that Viney might come and make any proposal he pleased; hoping for some chance-come expedient whereby he might screw out a little on account.

And so it followed that on the morning after his unsuccessful negotiation with Captain Nat, Dan Ogle found himself face to face with Henry Viney at that self-same spot on the bank-side where he had talked with Blind George.

Dan was surly; first because it was policy to say little, and to seem intractable, and again because, after the night's adventure, it came natural. "So you're Viney, are you?" he said. "Well, I ain't afraid o' you. I know about you. Blind George told me your game."

"Who said anything about afraid?" Viney protested, the eternal grin twitching nervously in his yellow cheeks. "We needn't talk about being afraid. It seems to me we can work together."

"O, does it? How?"

"Well, you know, you can't change 'em."

"What?"

"O, damn it, you know what I mean. The money—the notes."

"O, that's what you mean, is it? Well, s'pose I can't?"

"Well—of course—if you can't—eh? If you can't, they might be so much rags, eh?"

"P'raps they might—if I can't."

"But you know you can't," retorted the other, with a spasm of apprehension. "Else you'd have done it and—and got farther off."

"Well, p'raps I might. But that ain't all you come to say. Go on."

Viney thoughtfully scratched his lank cheek, peering sharply into Dan's face. "Things bein' what they are," he said, reflectively, "they're no more good to you than rags; not so much."

"All right. S'pose they ain't; you don't think I'm a-goin' to make you a present of 'em, do you?"

"Why no, I didn't think that. I'll pay—reasonable. But you must remember that they're no good to you at all—not worth rag price; so whatever you got 'ud be clear profit."

"Then how much clear profit will you give me?"

106

Viney's forefinger paused on his cheek, and his gaze, which had sunk to Dan Ogle's waistcoat, shot sharply again at his eyes. "Ten pounds," said Viney.

Dan chuckled, partly at the absurdity of the offer, partly because this bargaining for the unproducible began to amuse him. "Ten pound clear profit for me," he said, "an' eight hundred pound clear profit for you. That's your idea of a fair bit o' trade!"

"But it was mine first, and—and it's no good to you—you say so yourself!"

"No; nor no good to you neither—'cause why? You ain't got it!" Dan's chuckle became a grin. "If you'd ha' said a hundred, now——"

"What?"

"Why, then I'd ha' said four hundred. That's what I'd ha' said!"

"Four hundred? Why, you're mad! Besides I haven't got it— I've got nothing till I can change the notes; only the ten."

Dan saw the chance he had hoped for. "I'll make it dirt cheap," he said, "first an' last, no less an' no more. Will you give me fifty down for 'em when you've got 'em changed?"

"Yes, I will." Viney's voice was almost too eager.

"Straight? No tricks, eh?"

Viney was indignant at the suggestion. He scorned a trick.

"No hoppin' the twig with the whole lot, an' leavin' me in the cart?"

Viney was deeply hurt. He had never dreamed of such a thing.

"Very well, I'll trust you. Give us the tenner on account." Dan Ogle stuck out his hand carelessly; but it remained empty.

"I said I'd give fifty when they're changed," grinned Viney, knowingly.

"What? Well, I know that; an' not play no tricks. An' now when I ask you to pay first the ten you've got, you don't want to do it! That don't look like a chap that means to part straight and square, does it?"

Viney put his hand in his pocket. "All right," he said, "that's fair enough. Ten now an' forty when the paper's changed. Where's the paper?"

"O, I ain't got that about me just now," Dan replied airily. "Be here to-morrow, same time. But you can give me the ten now."

Viney's teeth showed unamiably through his grin. "Ah," he said; "I'll be here to-morrow with that, same time!"

"What?" It was Dan's honour that smarted now. "What? Won't trust me with ten, when I offer, free an' open, to trust you with forty? O, it's off then. I'm done. It's enough to make a man sick." And he turned loftily away.

Viney's grin waxed and waned, and he followed Dan with his eyes, thinking hard. Dan stole a look behind, and stopped.

"Look here," Viney said at last. "Look here. Let's cut it short. We can't sharp each other, and we're wasting time. You haven't got those notes."

Dan half-turned, and answered in a tone between question and retort. "O, haven't I?" he said.

"No; you haven't. See here; I'll give you five pounds if you'll show 'em to me. Only show 'em."

Dan was posed. "I said I hadn't got 'em about me," he said, rather feebly.

"No; nor can't get 'em. Can you? Cut it short."

Dan looked up and down, and rubbed his cap about his head. "I know where they are," he sulkily concluded.

"You know where they are, but you can't get 'em," Viney retorted with decision. "Can I get 'em?"

Dan glanced at him superciliously. "You?" he answered. "Lord, no."

"Can we get 'em together?"

Dan took to rubbing his cap about his head again, and staring very thoughtfully at the ground. Then he came a step nearer, and looked up. "Two might," he said, "if you'd see it through. With nerve."

Viney took him by the upper arm, and drew close. "We're the two," he said. "You know where the stuff is, and you say we can get it. We'll haggle no more. We're partners and we'll divide all we get. How's that?"

"How about Blind George?"

"Never mind Blind George—unless you want to make him a present. I don't. Blind George can fish for himself. He's shoved out. We'll do it, and we'll keep what we get. Now where are the notes? Who's got them?"

Dan Ogle stood silent a moment, considering. He looked over the bank toward the London streets, down on the grass at his feet, and then up at an adventurous lark, that sang nearer and still nearer the town smoke. Last he looked at Viney, and make up his mind. "Who's got 'em?" he repeated; "Cap'en Nat Kemp's got 'em."

"What? Cap'en——"

"Cap'en Nat Kemp's got 'em."

Viney took a step backward, turned his foot on the slope, and sat back on the bank, staring at Dan Ogle. "Cap'en Nat Kemp?" he said. "Cap'en Nat Kemp?"

"Ay; Cap'en Nat Kemp. The notes, an' the leather pocket-book; an' the photo; an' the whole kit. Marr's photo, ain't it, with his mother?"

"Yes," Viney answered. "When he was a boy. He wasn't a particular dutiful son, but he always carried it: for luck, or something. But—Cap'en Kemp! Where did he get them?"

Dan Ogle sat on the bank beside Viney, facing the river, and there told him the tale he had heard from Mrs. Grimes. Also he told him, with many suppressions, just as much of his own last night's adventure at the Hole in the Wall as made it plain that Captain Nat meant to stick to what he had got.

Viney heard it all in silence, and sat for a while with his head between his hands, thinking, and occasionally swearing. At last he looked up, and dropped one hand to his knee. "I'd have it out of him by myself," he said, "if it wasn't that I want to lie low a bit."

Dan grunted and nodded. "I know," he replied, "The Juno. I know about that."

Viney started. "What do you know about that?" he asked.

"Pretty well all you could tell me. I hear things, though I am lyin' up; but I heard before, too. Marr chattered like a poll-parrot."

Viney swore, and dropped his other hand. "Ay; so Blind George said. Well, there's nothing for me out of the insurance, and I'm going to let the creditors scramble for it themselves. There'd be awkward questions for me, with the books in the receiver's hands, and what not. So I'm not showing for a bit. Though," he added, thoughtfully, "I don't know that I mightn't try it, even now."

Dan's eyes grew sharp. "We're doin' this together, Mr. Viney," he said. "You'd better not go tryin' things without me; I mightn't like it. I ain't a nice man to try games on with; one's tried a game over this a'ready, mind."

"I'm trying no games," Viney protested. "Tell us your way, if you don't want to hear about mine."

Dan Ogle was sitting with his chin on his doubled fists, gazing thoughtfully at the muddy river. "My way's rough," he replied, "but it's thorough. An' it wipes off scores. I owe Cap'en Nat one."

Viney looked curiously at his companion. "Well?" he said.

"An' there'd be more in it than eight hundred an' ten. P'raps a lump more."

"How?" Viney's eyes widened.

"Umph." Dan was silent a moment. Then he turned and looked Viney in the eyes. "Are you game?" he asked. "You ain't a faintin' sort, are you? You oughtn't to be, seein' you was a ship's officer."

109

Viney's mouth closed tight. "No," he said; "I don't think I am. What is it?"

Dan Ogle looked intently in his face for a few seconds, and then said: "Only him an' the kid sleeps in the house."

Viney started. "You don't mean breaking in?" he exclaimed. "I won't do that; it's too—too——"

"Ah, too risky, of course," Dan replied, with a curl of the lip. "But I don't mean breakin' in. Nothing like it. But tell me first; s'pose breakin' in wasn't risky; s'pose you knew you'd get away safe, with the stuff. Would you do it then?" And he peered keenly at Viney's face.

Viney frowned. "That don't matter," he said, "if it ain't the plan. S'pose I would?"

"Ha-ha! that'll do! I know your sort. Not that I blame you about the busting—it 'ud take two pretty tough 'uns to face Cap'en Nat, I can tell you. But now see here. Will you come with me, an' knock at his side door to-night, after the place is shut?"

"Knock? And what then?"

"I'll tell you. You know the alley down to the stairs?"

"Yes."

"Black as pitch at night, with a row o' posts holding up the house. Now when everybody's gone an' he's putting out the lights, you go an' tap at the door."

"Well?"

"You tap at the door, an' he'll come. You're alone—see? I stand back in the dark, behind a post. He never sees me. 'Good evenin',' says you. 'I just want a word with you, if you'll step out.' And so he does."

"And what then?"

"Nothing else—not for you; that's all your job. Easy enough, ain't it?"

Viney turned where he sat, and stared fixedly at his confederate's face. "And then—then—what——"

"Then I come on. He don't know I'm there—behind him."

Viney's mouth opened a little, but with no grin; and for a minute the two sat, each looking in the other's face. Then said Viney, with a certain shrinking: "No, no; not that. It's hanging, you know; it's hanging—for both."

Dan laughed—an ugly laugh, and short. "It ain't hanging for that," he said; "it's hanging for gettin' caught. An' where's the chance o' that? We take our own time, and the best place you ever see for a job like that, river handy at the end an' all; an' everything settled beforehand. Safe a job as ever I see. Look at me. I ain't hung

110

yet, am I? But I've took my chances, an' took 'em when it wasn't safe, like as this is."

Viney stared at vacancy, like a man in a brown study; and his dry tongue passed slowly along his drier lips.

"As for bein' safe," Dan went on, "what little risk there is, is for me. You're all right. We don't know each other. Not likely. How should you know I was hidin' there in the dark when you went to speak to Cap'en Nat Kemp? Come to that, it might ha' been you outed instead o' your friend what you was talkin' so sociable with. An' there's more there than what's in the pocket-book. Remember that. There's a lump more than that."

Viney rubbed his mouth with the back of his hand. "How do you know?" he asked, huskily.

"How do I know? How did I know about the pocket-book an' the notes? I ain't been the best o' pals with my sister, but she couldn't ha' been there all this time without my hearing a thing or two about Cap'en Nat; to say nothing of what everybody knows as knows anything about him. Money? O' course there's money in the place; no telling how much; an' watches, an' things, as he buys. P'raps twice that eight hundred, an' more."

Viney's eyes were growing sharper—growing eager. "It sounds all right," he remarked, a little less huskily. "Especially if there's more in it than the eight hundred. But—but—are you—you know—sure about it?"

"You leave that to me. I'll see after my department, an' yours is easy enough. Come, it's a go, ain't it?"

"But perhaps he'll make a row—call out, or something."

"He ain't the sort o' chap to squeal; an' if he was he wouldn't—not the way I'm goin' to do it. You'll see."

"An' there's the boy—what about him?"

"O, the kid? Upstairs. He's no account, after we've outed Cap'en Nat. No more'n a tame rabbit. An' we'll have all night to turn the place over, if we want it—though we shan't. We'll be split out before the potman comes: fifty mile apart, with full pockets, an' nobody a ha'porth the wiser."

Viney bit at his fingers, and his eyes lifted and sank, quick and keen, from the ground to Ogle's face, and back again. But it was enough, and he asked for no more persuasion. Willing murderers both, they set to planning details: what Viney should say, if it were necessary to carry the talk with Captain Nat beyond the first sentence or so; where they must meet; and the like. And here, on Viney's motion, a change was made as regarded time. Not this immediate night, but the night following, was resolved on for the

111

stroke that should beggar the Hole in the Wall of money and of life. For to Viney it seemed desirable, first, to get his belongings away from his present lodgings, for plain reasons; so as to throw off Blind George, and so as to avoid flight from a place where he was known, on the very night of the crime. This it were well to do at once; yet, all unprepared as he was, he could not guess what delays might intervene; and so for all reasons Captain Nat and the child were reprieved for twenty-four hours.

Thus in full terms the treaty was made. Dan Ogle, shrink as he might from Captain Nat face to face (as any ruffian in Blue Gate would), was as ready to stab him in the back for vengeance as for gain. For he was conscious that never in all his years of bullying and scoundrelism had he cut quite so poor a figure in face of any man as last night in face of Captain Nat. As to the gain, it promised to be large, and easy in the getting; and for his sister, now that she could help no more,—she could as readily be flung out of the business as Blind George. The opportunity was undeniable. A better place for the purpose than the alley leading to the head of Hole-in-the-Wall Stairs could never have been planned. Once the house was shut, and the potman gone, no more was needed than to see the next police patrol go by, and the thing was done. Here was the proper accomplice too: a man known to Captain Nat, and one with whom he would readily speak; and, in Ogle's eyes, the business was no more than a common stroke of his trade, with an uncommon prospect of profit. As for Viney, money was what he wanted, and here it could be made, as it seemed, with no great risk. It was surer, far, than going direct to Captain Nat and demanding the money under the old threat. That was a little outworn, and, indeed, was not so substantial a bogey as it might seem in the eyes of Captain Nat, for years remorseful, and now apprehensive for his grandchild's sake; for the matter was old, and evidence scarce, except Viney's own, which it would worse than inconvenience him to give. So that a large demand might break down; while here, as he was persuaded, was the certainty of a greater gain, which was the main thing. And if any shadow of scruple against direct and simple murder remained, it vanished in the reflection that not he, but Ogle, would be the perpetrator, as well as the contriver. For himself, he would but be opening an innocent conversation with Kemp. So Viney told himself; and so desire and conscience are made to run coupled, all the world over, and all time through.

All being appointed, the two men separated. They stood up, they looked about them, over the Lea and over the ragged field; and they shook hands.

CHAPTER XXIII
ON THE COP

It was morning still, as Viney went away over the Cop; and, when he had vanished beyond the distant group of little houses, Dan Ogle turned and crept lazily into his shelter: there to make what dinner he might from the remnant of the food that Mag had brought him the evening before; and to doze away the time on his bed of dusty sacks, till she should bring more in the evening to come. He would have given much for a drink, for since his retreat to Kemp's Wharf the lime had penetrated clothes and skin and had invaded his very vitals. More particularly it had invaded his throat; and the pint or so of beer that Mag brought in a bottle was not enough to do more than aggravate the trouble. But no drink was there, and no money to buy one; else he might well have ventured out to a public-house, now that the police sought him no more. As for Grimes of the wharf (who had been growing daily more impatient of Dan's stay), he offered no better relief than a surly reference to the pump. So there was nothing for it but to sit and swear; with the consolation that this night should be his last at Kemp's Wharf.

Sunlight came with the afternoon, and speckled the sluggish Lea; then the shadow of the river wall fell on the water and it was dull again; and the sun itself grew duller, and lower, and larger, in the haze of the town. If Dan Ogle had climbed the bank, and had looked across the Cop now, he would have seen Blind George, stick in hand, feeling his way painfully among hummocks and ditches in the distance. Dan, however, was expecting nobody, and he no longer kept watch on all comers, so that Blind George neared unnoted. He gained the lime-strewn road at last, and walked with more confidence. Up and over the bank, and down on the side next the river, he went so boldly that one at a distance would never have guessed him blind; for on any plain road he had once traversed he was never at fault; and he turned with such readiness at the proper spot, and so easily picked his way to the shed, that Dan had scarce more warning than could bring him as far as the door, where they met.

"Dan!" the blind man said; "Dan, old pal! It's you I can hear, I'll bet, ain't it? Where are ye?" And he groped for a friendly grip.

Dan Ogle was taken by surprise, and a little puzzled. Still, he could do no harm by hearing what Blind George had to say; so he answered: "All right. What is it?"

Guided by the sound, Blind George straightway seized Dan's arm; for this was his way of feeling a speaker's thoughts while he heard his words. "He's gone," he said, "gone clean. Do you know where?"

Dan glared into the sightless eye and shook his captured arm roughly. "Who?" he asked.

"Viney. Did you let him have the stuff?"

"What stuff? When?"

"What stuff? That's a rum thing to ask. Unless—O!" George dropped his voice and put his face closer. "Anybody to hear?" he whispered.

"No."

"Then why ask what stuff? You didn't let him have it this morning, did you?"

"Dunno what you mean. Never seen him this morning."

Blind George retracted his head with a jerk, and a strange look grew on his face: a look of anger and suspicion; strange because the great colourless eye had no part in it. "Dan," he said, slowly, "them ain't the words of a pal—not of a faithful pal, they ain't. It's a damn lie!"

"Lie yourself!" retorted Dan, thrusting him away. "Let go my arm, go on!"

"I knew he was coming," Blind George went on, "an' I follered up, an' waited behind them houses other side the Cop. I want my whack, I do. I heared him coming away, an' I called to him, but he scuttled off. I know his step as well as what another man 'ud know his face. I'm a poor blind bloke, but I ain't a fool. What's your game, telling me a lie like that?"

He was standing off from the door now, angry and nervously alert. Dan growled, and then said: "You clear out of it. You come to me first from Viney, didn't you? Very well, you're his pal in this. Go and talk to him about it."

"I've been—that's where I've come from. I've been to his lodgings in Chapman Street, an' he's gone. Said he'd got a berth aboard ship—a lie. Took his bag an' cleared, soon as ever he could get back from here. He's on for doing me out o' my whack, arter I put it all straight for him—that's about it. You won't put me in the cart, Dan, arter all I done! Where's he gone?"

"I dunno nothing about him, I tell you," Dan answered angrily. "You sling your hook, or I'll make ye!"

114

"Dan," said the blind man, in a voice between appeal and threat; "Dan, I didn't put you away, when I found you was here!"

"Put me away? You? You can go an' try it now, if you like. I ain't wanted; they won't have me. An' if they would—how long 'ud you last, next time you went into Blue Gate? Or even if you didn't go, eh? How long would a man last, that had both his eyes to see with, eh?" And indeed Blind George knew, as well as Dan himself, that London was unhealthy for any traitor to the state and liberty of Blue Gate. "How long would he last? You try it."

"Who wants to try it? I on'y want to know——"

"Shut your mouth, Blind George, an' get out o' this place!" Ogle cried, fast losing patience, and making a quick step forward. "Go, or you'll be lame as well as blind, if I get hold o' ye!"

Blind George backed involuntarily, but his blank face darkened and twisted devilishly, and he gripped his stick like a cudgel. "Ah, I'm blind, ain't I? Mighty bold with a blind man, ain't ye? If my eyes was like yours, or you was blind as me, you'd——"

"Go!" roared Dan furiously, with two quick steps. "Go!"

The blind man backed as quickly, fiercely brandishing his stick. "I'll go—just as far as suits me, Dan Ogle!" he cried. "I ain't goin' to be done out o' what's mine! One of ye's got away, but I'll stick to the other! Keep off! I'll stick to ye till—keep off!"

As Dan advanced, the stick, flourished at random, fell on his wrist with a crack, and in a burst of rage he rushed at the blind man, and smote him down with blow on blow. Blind George, beaten to a heap, but cowed not at all, howled like a wild beast, and struck madly with his stick. The stick reached its mark more than once, and goaded Ogle to a greater fury. He punched and kicked at the plunging wretch at his feet: who, desperate and unflinching, with his mouth spluttering blood and curses, never ceased to strike back as best he might.

At the noise Grimes came hurrying from his office. For a moment he stood astonished, and then he ran and caught Dan by the arm. "I won't have it!" he cried. "If you want to fight you go somewhere else. You—why—why, damme, the man's blind!"

Favoured by the interruption, Blind George crawled a little off, smearing his hand through the blood on his face, breathless and battered, but facing his enemy still, with unabashed malevolence. For a moment Ogle turned angrily on Grimes, but checked himself, and let fall his hands. "Blind?" he snarled. "He'll be dead too, if he don't keep that stick to hisself; that's what he'll be!"

The blind man got on his feet, and backed away, smearing the grisly face as he went. "Ah! hold him back!" he cried, with a double mouthful of oaths. "Hold him hack for his own sake! I ain't done with you, Dan Ogle, not yet! Fight? Ah, I'll fight you—an' fight you level! I mean it! I do! I'll fight you level afore I've done with you! Dead I'll be, will I? Not afore you, an' not afore I've paid you!" So he passed over the bank, threatening fiercely.

"Look here," said Grimes to Ogle, "this ends this business. I've had enough o' you. You find some other lodgings."

"All right," Ogle growled. "I'm going: after to-night."

"I dunno why I was fool enough to let you come," Grimes pursued. "An' when I did, I never said your pals was to come too. I remember that blind chap now; I see him in Blue Gate, an' I don't think much of him. An' there was another chap this morning. Up to no good, none of ye; an' like as not to lose me my job. So I'll find another use for that shed, see?"

"All right," the other sulkily repeated. "I tell ye I'm going: after to-night."

CHAPTER XXIV
ON THE COP

Once he had cut clear from his lodgings without delay and trouble, Viney fell into an insupportable nervous impatience, which grew with every minute. His reasons for the day's postponement now seemed wholly insufficient: it must have been, he debated with himself, that the first shock of the suggestion had driven him to the nearest excuse to put the job off, as it were a dose of bitter physic. But now that the thing was resolved upon, and nothing remained to do in preparation, the suspense of inactivity became intolerable, and grew to torment. It was no matter of scruple or compunction; of that he never dreamed. But the enterprise was dangerous and novel, and, as the vacant hours passed, he imagined new perils and dreamed a dozen hangings. Till at last, as night came on, he began to fear that his courage could not hold out the time; and, since there was now no reason for delay, he ended with a resolve to get the thing over and the money in his pockets that same night, if it were possible. And with that view he set out for the Cop....

Meantime no nervousness troubled his confederate; for him it was but a good stroke of trade, with a turn of revenge in it; and the

116

penniless interval mattered nothing—could be slept off, in fact, more or less, since there was nothing else to do.

The sun sank below London, and night came slow and black over the marshes and the Cop. Grimes, rising from the doorstep of his office, knocked the last ashes from his pipe and passed indoors. Dan Ogle, sitting under the lee of his shed, found no comfort in his own empty pipe, and no tobacco in his empty pocket. He rose, stretched his arms, and looked across the Lea and the Cop. He could see little or nothing, for the dark was closing on him fast. "Blind man's holiday," muttered Dan Ogle; and he turned in for a nap on his bed of sacks.

A sulky red grew up into the darkening western sky, as though the extinguished sun were singeing all the world's edge. So one saw London's nimbus from this point every night, and saw below it the scattered spangle of lights that were the suburban sentries of the myriads beyond. The Cop and the marshes lay pitch-black, and nothing but the faint lap of water hinted that a river divided them.

Here, where an hour's habit blotted the great hum of London from the consciousness, sounds were few. The perseverance of the lapping water forced a groan now and again from the moorings of an invisible barge lying by the wharf; and as often a ghostly rustle rose on the wind from an old willow on the farther bank. And presently, more distinct than either, came a steady snore from the shed where Dan Ogle lay....

A rustle, that was not of any tree, began when the snore was at its steadiest; a gentle rustle indeed, where something, some moving shadow in the black about it, crept over the river wall. Clearer against a faint patch, which had been white with lime in daylight, the figure grew to that of a man; a man moving in that murky darkness with an amazing facility, address, and quietness. Down toward the riverside he went, and there stooping, dipped into the water some small coarse bag of cloth, that hung in his hand. Then he rose, and, after a listening pause, turned toward the shed whence came the snore.

With three steps and a pause, and three steps more, he neared the door: the stick he carried silently skimming the ground before him, his face turned upward, his single eye rolling blankly at the sky that was the same for him at night or noon; and the dripping cloth he carried diffused a pungent smell, as of wetted quick-lime. So, creeping and listening, he reached the door. Within, the snore was regular and deep.

Nothing held the door but a latch, such as is lifted by a finger thrust through a hole. He listened for a moment with his ear at this

117

hole, and then, with infinite precaution, inserted his finger, and lifted the latch....

Up by the George Tavern, beyond Stepney, Henry Viney was hastening along the Commercial Road to call Dan Ogle to immediate business. Ahead of him by a good distance, Musky Mag hurried in the same direction, bearing food in a saucer and handkerchief, and beer in a bottle. But hurry as they might, here was a visitor well ahead of both....

The door opened with something of a jar, and with that there was a little choke in the snore, and a moment's silence. Then the snore began again, deep as before. Down on his knees went Dan Ogle's visitor, and so crawled into the deep of the shed.

He had been gone no more than a few seconds, when the snore stopped. It stopped with a thump and a gasp, and a sudden buffeting of legs and arms; and in the midst arose a cry: a cry of so hideous an agony that Grimes the wharf-keeper, snug in his first sleep fifty yards away, sprang erect and staring in bed, and so sat motionless for half a minute ere he remembered his legs, and thrust them out to carry him to the window. And the dog on the wharf leapt the length of its chain, answering the cry with a torrent of wild barks.

Floundering and tumbling against the frail boards of the shed, the two men came out at the door in a struggling knot: Ogle wrestling and striking at random, while the other, cunning with a life's blindness, kept his own head safe, and hung as a dog hangs to a bull. His hands gripped his victim by ear and hair, while the thumbs still drove at the eyes the mess of smoking lime that clung and dripped about Ogle's head. It trickled burning through his hair, and it blistered lips and tongue, as he yelled and yelled again in the extremity of his anguish. Over they rolled before the doorway; and Ogle, snatching now at last instead of striking, tore away the hands from his face.

"Fight you level, Dan Ogle, fight you level now!" Blind George gasped between quick breaths. "Hit me now you're blind as me! Hit me! Knock me down! Eh?"

Quickly he climbed to his feet, and aimed a parting blow with the stick that hung from his wrist. "Dead?" he whispered hoarsely. "Not afore I've paid you! No!"

He might have stayed to strike again, but his own hands were blistered in the struggle, and he hastened off toward the bank, there to wash them clear of the slaking lime. Away on the wharf the dog was yelping and choking on its chain like a mad thing.

Screaming still, with a growing hoarseness, and writhing

118

where he lay, the blinded wretch scratched helplessly at the reeking lime that scorched his skin and seared his eyes almost to the brain. Grimes came running in shirt and trousers, and, as soon as he could find how matters stood, turned and ran again for oil. "Good God!" he said. "Lime in his eyes! Slaking lime! Why—why—it must be the blind chap! It must! Fight him level, he said—an' he's blinded him!..."

There was a group of people staring at the patients' door of the Accident Hospital when Viney reached the spot. He was busy enough with his own thoughts, but he stopped, and stared also, involuntarily. The door was an uninteresting object, however, after all, and he turned: to find himself face to face with one he well remembered. It was the limy man he had followed from Blue Gate to the Hole in the Wall, and then lost sight of.

Grimes recognised Viney at once as Ogle's visitor of the morning. "That's a pal o' yourn just gone in there," he said.

Viney was taken aback. "A pal?" he asked. "What pal?"

"Ogle—Dan Ogle. He's got lime in his eyes, an' blinded."

"Lime? Blinded? How?"

"I ain't goin' to say nothing about how—I dunno, an' 'tain't my business. He's got it, anyhow. There's a woman in there along of him—his wife, I b'lieve, or something. You can talk to her about it, if you like, when she comes out. I've got nothing to do with it."

Grimes had all the reluctance of his class to be "mixed up" in any matter likely to involve trouble at a police-court; and what was more, he saw himself possibly compromised in the matter of Ogle's stay at the Wharf. But Viney was so visibly concerned by the news that soon the wharf-keeper relented a little—thinking him maybe no such bad fellow after all, since he was so anxious about his friend. "I've heard said," he added presently in a lower tone, "I've heard said it was a blind chap done it out o' spite; but of course I dunno; not to say myself; on'y what I heard, you see. I don't think they'll let you in; but you might see the woman. They won't let her stop long, 'specially takin' on as she was."

Indeed it was not long ere Musky Mag emerged, reluctant and pallid, trembling at the mouth, staring but seeing nothing. Grimes took her by the arm and led her aside, with Viney. "Here's a friend o' Dan's," Grimes said, not unkindly, giving the woman a shake of the arm. "He wants to know how he's gettin' on."

"What's 'nucleate?" she asked hoarsely, with a dull look in Viney's face. "What's 'nucleate? I heard a doctor say to let 'im rest to-night an' 'nucleate in the mornin'. What's 'nucleate?"

"Some sort o' operation," Grimes hazarded. "Did they say anything else?"

"Blinded," the woman answered weakly. "Blinded. But the pain's eased with the oil."

"What did he say?" interposed Viney, fullest of his own concerns. "Did he say someone did it?"

"He told me about it—whispered. But I shan't say nothing; nor him, not till he comes out."

"I say—he mustn't get talkin' about it," Viney said, anxiously. "It—it'll upset things. Tell him when you see him. Here, listen." He took her aside out of Grimes's hearing. "It wouldn't do," he said, "it wouldn't do to have anybody charged or anything just now. We've got something big to pull off. I say—I ought to see him, you know. Can't I see him? But there—someone might know me. No. But you must tell him. He mustn't go informing, or anything like that, not yet. Tell him, won't you?"

"Chargin'? Infornin'?" Mag answered, with contempt in her shaking voice. "'Course 'e wouldn't go informin', not Dan. Dan ain't that sort—'e looks arter hisself, 'e does; 'e don't go chargin' people. Not if 'e was dyin'."

Indeed Viney did not sufficiently understand the morals of Blue Gate: where to call in the aid of the common enemy, the police, was a foul trick to which none would stoop. In Blue Gate a man inflicted his own punishments, and to ask aid of the police was worse than mean and scandalous: it was weak; and that in a place where the weak "did not last," as the phrase went. It was the one restraint, the sole virtue of the place, enduring to death; and like some other virtues, in some other places, it had its admixture of necessity; for everybody was "wanted" in turn, and to call for the help of a policeman who might, as likely as not, begin by seizing oneself by the collar, would even have been poor policy: bad equally for the individual and for the community. So that to resort to the law's help in any form was classed with "narking" as the unpardonable sin.

"You're sure o' that, are you?" asked Viney, apprehensively.

"Sure? 'Course I'm sure. Dunno what sort o' chap you take 'im for. 'E's no nark. An' besides—'e can't. There's other things, an'——"

She turned away with a sigh that was near a sob, and her momentary indignation lapsed once more into anxious grief.

Viney went off with his head confused and his plans in the melting-pot. Ogle's scheme was gone by the board, and alone he could scarce trust himself in any enterprise so desperate. What

120

should he do now? Make what terms he might with Captain Nat? Need was pressing; but he must think.

CHAPTER XXV
STEPHEN'S TALE

I have said something of the change in my grandfather's habits after the news of the loss of the Juno and my father's death; something but not all. Not only was he abstracted in manner and aged in look, but he grew listless in matters of daily life, and even doubtful and infirm of purpose: an amazing thing in him, whose decision of character had made his a corner of the world in which his will was instant law. And with it, and through it all, I could feel that I was the cause. "It ain't the place for you, Stevy, never the place for you," he would say, wistful and moody; wholly disregarding my protests, which I doubt he even heard. "I've put one thing right," he said once, thinking aloud, as I sat on his knee; "but it ain't enough; it ain't enough." And I was sure that he was thinking of the watches and spoons.

As to that matter, people with valuables had wholly ceased from coming to the private compartment. But the pale man still sat in his corner, and Joe the potman still supplied the drink he neglected. His uneasiness grew less apparent in a day or so; but he remained puzzled and curious, though no doubt well enough content with this, the most patent example of Grandfather Nat's irresolution.

As for Mr. Cripps, that deliberate artist's whole practice of life was disorganised by Captain Nat's indifference, and he was driven to depend for the barest necessaries on the casual generosity of the bar. In particular he became the client of the unsober sailor I have spoken of already: the disciplinarian, who had roared confirmation of my grandfather's orders when the man of the silver spoons got his dismissal. This sailor was old in the ways of Wapping, as in the practice of soaking, it would seem, and he gave himself over to no crimp. Being ashore, with money to spend, he preferred to come alone to the bar of The Hole in the Wall, and spend it on himself, getting full measure for every penny. Beyond his talent of ceaselessly absorbing liquor without becoming wholly drunk, and a shrewd eye for his correct change, he exhibited the single personal characteristic of a very demonstrative respect for Captain Nat Kemp. He would confirm my grandfather's slightest order with shouts and threats, which as often as not were only to be quelled by a shout or a threat from my grandfather himself, a thing of instant effect, however. "Ay, ay, sir!" the man would answer, and humbly return to his pot. "Cap'en's orders" he would sometimes add, with a wink and a hoarse whisper to a chance neighbour. "Always 'bey cap'en's orders. Knowed 'em both, father an' son."

So that Mr. Cripps's ready acquiescence in whatever was said loudly, and in particular his own habit of blandiloquence, led to a sort of agreement between the two, and an occasional drink at the sailor's expense.

But, meantime, his chief patron was grown so abstracted from considerations of the necessities of genius, so impervious to hints, so deaf to all suggestion of grant-in-aid, that Mr. Cripps was driven to a desperate and dramatic stroke. One morning he appeared in the bar carrying the board for the sign; no tale of a board, no description or account of a board, no estimate or admeasurement of a board; but the actual, solid, material board itself.

By what expedient he had acquired it did not fully appear, and, indeed, with him, cash and credit were about equally scarce. But upon one thing he most vehemently insisted: that he dared not return home without the money to pay for it. The ravening creditor would be lying in wait at the corner of his street.

Mr. Cripps's device for breaking through Captain Nat's abstraction succeeded beyond all calculation. For my grandfather laid hands on Mr. Cripps and the board together, and hauled both straightway into the skippers' parlour at the back.

"There's the board," he said with decision, "an' there's you. Where's the paints an' brushes?"

Mr. Cripps's stock of paints was low, it seemed, or exhausted. His brushes were at home and—his creditor was at the corner of the street.

"If I could take the proceeds"—Mr. Cripps began; but Grandfather Nat interrupted. "Here's you, an' here's the board, an' we'll soon get the tools: I'll send for 'em or buy new. Here, Joe! Joe'll get 'em. You say what you want, an' he'll fetch 'em. Here you are, an' here you stick, an' do my signboard!"

Mr. Cripps dared not struggle for his liberty, and indeed a promise of his meals at the proper hours reconciled him to my grandfather's defiance of Magna Charta. So the skipper's parlour became his studio; and there he was left in company with his materials, a pot of beer, and a screw of tobacco. I much desired to see the painting, but it was ruled that Mr. Cripps must not be disturbed. I think I must have restrained my curiosity for an hour at least, ere I ventured on tip-toe to peep through a little window used for the passing in and out of drinks and empty glasses. Here my view was somewhat obstructed by Mr. Cripps's pot, which, being empty, he had placed upside down in the opening, as a polite intimation to whomsoever it might concern; but I could see that Mr. Cripps's labours having proceeded so far as the selection of a convenient chair, he was now taking relaxation in profound slumber. So I went away and said nothing.

When at last he was disturbed by the arrival of his dinner, Mr. Cripps regained consciousness with a sudden bounce that almost deposited him on the floor.

"Conception," he gasped, rubbing his eyes, "conception, an' meditation, an' invention, is what you want in a job like this!"

"Ah," replied my grandfather grimly, "that's all, is it? Then common things like dinner don't matter. Perhaps Joe'd better take it away?"

But it seemed that Mr. Cripps wanted his dinner too. He had it; but Grandfather Nat made it clear that he should consider meditation wholly inconsistent with tea. So that, in course of the afternoon, Mr. Cripps was fain to paint the board white, and so earn a liberal interval of rest, while it dried. And at night he went away home without the price of the board, but, instead, a note to the effect that the amount was payable on application to Captain Kemp at the Hole in the Wall, Wapping. This note was the production, after three successive failures, of my own pen, and to me a matter of great pride and delight; so that I was sadly disappointed to observe that Mr. Cripps received it with emotions of a wholly different character.

Next morning Mr. Cripps returned to durance with another pot and another screw of tobacco. Grandfather Nat had business in the Minories in the matter of a distiller's account; and for this reason divers injunctions, stipulations, and warnings were entered into and laid upon Mr. Cripps before his departure. As for instance:—

It was agreed that Mr. Cripps should remain in the skipper's parlour.

Also (after some trouble) that no exception should be made to the foregoing stipulation, even in the event of Mr. Cripps feeling it necessary to go out somewhere to study a brick wall (or the hole in it) from nature.

Nor even if he felt overcome by the smell of paint.

Agreed, however: that an exception be granted in the event of the house being on fire.

Further: this with more trouble: that one pot of beer before dinner is enough for any man seriously bent on the pursuit of art.

Moreover: that the board must not be painted white again.

Lastly: that the period of invention and meditation be considered at an end; and that sleep on Mr. Cripps's part be regarded as an acknowledgment that meals are over for the day.

These articles being at length agreed and confirmed, and Mr. Cripps having been duly witnessed to make certain marks with charcoal on the white board, as a guarantee of good faith, Grandfather Nat and I set out for the Minories.

His moodiness notwithstanding, it was part of his new habit to keep me near him as much as possible, day and night, with a sort of wistful jealousy. So we walked hand in hand over the swing bridge, past Paddy's Goose, into the Highway, and on through that same pageant of romance and squalor. The tradesmen at their doors saluted Grandfather Nat with a subdued regard, as I had observed most people to do since the news of Juno's wreck. Indeed that disaster was very freely spoken of, all along the waterside, as a deliberate scuttling, and it was felt that Captain Nat could lay his bereavement to something worse than the fair chance of the seas. Such things were a part of the daily talk by the Docks, and here all the familiar features were present; while it was especially noted that nothing had been seen of Viney since the news came. He meant to lie safe, said the gossips; since, as a bankrupt, he stood to gain nothing by the insurance.

One tradesman alone, a publican just beyond Blue Gate, greeted my grandfather noisily, but he was thoughtless with the pride of commercial achievement. For he was enlarging his bar, a large one already, by the demolition of the adjoining shop, and he was anxious to exhibit and explain his designs.

"Why, good mornin', Cap'en," cried the publican, from amid scaffold poles and brick-dust. "You're a stranger lately. See what I'm doin'? Here: come in here an' look. How's this, eh? Another pair o' doors just over there, an' the bar brought round like so, an' that for Bottle an' Jug, and throw the rest into Public Bar. Eh?"

The party wall had already been removed, and the structure above rested on baulks and beams. The bar was screened off now from the place of its enlargement by nothing but canvas and tarpaulin, and my grandfather and his acquaintance stood with their backs to this, to survey the work of the builders.

Waiting by my grandfather's side while he talked, I was soon aware that business was brisk in the bar beyond the canvas; and I listened idly to the hum of custom and debate. Suddenly I grew aware of a voice I knew—an acrid voice just within the canvas.

"Then if you're useless, I ain't," said the voice, "an' I shan't let it drop." And indeed it was Mrs. Grimes who spoke.

I looked up quickly at Grandfather Nat, but he was interested in his discussion, and plainly had not heard. Mrs. Grimes's declaration drew a growling answer in a man's voice, wholly indistinct; and I found a patch in the canvas, with a loose corner, which afforded a peep-hole.

Mrs. Grimes was nearest, with her back to the canvas, so that her skirts threatened to close my view. Opposite her were two persons, in the nearest of whom I was surprised to recognise the coarse-faced woman I had seen twice before: once when she came asking confused questions to Grandfather Nat about the man who sold a watch, and once when she fainted at the inquest, and Mrs. Grimes was too respectable to stay near her. The woman looked sorrowful and drawn about the eyes and cheeks, and she held to the arm of a tall, raw-boned man. His face was seamed with ragged and blistered skin, and he wore a shade over the hollows where now, peeping upward, I could see no eyes, but shut and sunken lids; so that at first it was hard to recognise the fellow who had been talking to this same coarse-faced woman by Blue Gate, when she left him to ask those questions of my grandfather; and indeed I should never have remembered him but that the woman brought him to my mind.

It was this man whose growling answer I had heard. Now Mrs. Grimes spoke again. "All my fault from the beginning?" she said. "O yes, I like that: because I wanted to keep myself respectable! My fault or not, I shan't wait any longer for you. If I ain't to have it, you shan't. An' if I can't get the money I can get something else."

The man growled again and swore, and beat his stick impotently on the floor. "You're a fool," he said. "Can't you wait till I'm a bit straight? You an' your revenge! Pah! When there's money to be had!"

"Not much to be had your way, it seems, the mess you've made of it; an' precious likely to do any better now, ain't you? An' as to money—well there's rewards given——"

Grandfather Nat's hand fell on my cap, and startled me. He had congratulated his friend, approved his plans, made a few suggestions, and now was ready to resume the walk. He talked still as he took my hand, and stood thus for a few minutes by the door, exchanging views with the publican on the weather, the last ships

125

in, and the state of trade. I heard one more growl, louder and angrier than the others, from beyond the screen, and a sharper answer, and then there was a movement and the slam of a door; and I got over the step, and stretched my grandfather's arm and my own to see Mrs. Grimes go walking up the street.

When we were free of the publican, I told Grandfather Nat that I had seen Mrs. Grimes in the bar. He made so indifferent a reply that I said nothing of the conversation I had overheard; for indeed I knew nothing of its significance. And so we went about our business.

CHAPTER XXVI
STEPHEN'S TALE

On our way home we were brought to a stand at the swing bridge, which lay open to let through a ship. We were too late for the perilous lock; for already the capstans were going, and the ship's fenders were squeaking and groaning against the masonry. So we stood and waited till fore, main, and mizzen had crawled by; and then I was surprised to observe, foremost and most impatient among the passengers on the opposite side, Mr. Cripps.

The winches turned, and the bridge swung; and my surprise grew, when I perceived that Mr. Cripps made no effort to avoid Grandfather Nat, but hurried forward to meet him.

"Well," said my grandfather gruffly, "house on fire?"

"No, sir—no. But I thought——"

"Sign done?"

"No, Cap'en, not done exactly. But I just got curious noos, an' so I come to meet you."

"What's the news?"

"Not p'raps exactly as you might say noos, sir, but information—information that's been transpired to me this mornin'. More or less unique information, so to say,—uncommon unique; much uniquer than usual."

With these repetitions Mr. Cripps looked hard in my grandfather's eyes, as one does who wishes to break news, or lead up to a painful subject. "What's it all about?" asked Grandfather Nat.

126

"The Juno."

"Well?"

"She was scuttled wilful, Cap'en Kemp, scuttled wilful by Beecher. It's more'n rumour or scandal: it's plain evidence."

My grandfather looked fixedly at Mr. Cripps. "What's the plain evidence?" he asked.

"That chap that's been so much in the bar lately," Mr. Cripps answered, his eyes wide with the importance of his discovery. "The chap that soaks so heavy, an' shouts at any one you order out. He was aboard the Juno on the voyage out, an' he deserted at Monte Video to a homeward bound ship."

"Then he doesn't know about the wreck." I thought my grandfather made this objection almost eagerly.

"No, Cap'en; but he deserted 'cos he said he preferred bein' on a ship as was meant to come back, an' one as had some grub aboard—him an' others. Beecher tried to pile 'em up time an' again; an' says the chap—Conolly's his name—says he, anything as went wrong aboard the Juno was Beecher's doin'; which was prophesied in the fo'c'sle a score o' times 'fore she got to Monte Video. An'—an' Conolly said more." Mr. Cripps stole another sidelong glance at Grandfather Nat. "Confidential to me this mornin', Conolly said more."

"What?"

"He said it was the first officer, your son, Cap'en, as prevented the ship bein' piled up on the voyage out, an' all but knocked Beecher down once. An' he said they was near fightin' half the time he was with 'em, an' he said—surprisin' solemn too—solemn as a man could as was half drunk—that after what he'd seen an' heard, anything as happened to the first mate was no accident, or anything like it. That's what he said, cap'en, confidential to me this mornin'."

We were walking along together now; and Mr. Cripps seemed puzzled that his information produced no more startling effect on my grandfather. The old man's face was pale and hard, but there was no sign of surprise; which was natural, seeing that this was no news, as Mr. Cripps supposed, but merely confirmation.

"He said there was never any skipper so partic'ler about the boats an' davits bein' kep' in order as Beecher was that trip," Mr. Cripps proceeded. "An' he kep' his own life-belt wonderful handy. As for the crew, they kep' their kit-bags packed all the time; they could see enough for that. An' he said there was some as could say more'n he could."

We came in view of the Hole in the Wall, and Mr. Cripps stopped short. "He don't know I'm tellin' you this," he said. "He

127

came in the skipper's room with a drink, an' got talkin' confidential. He's very close about it. You know what sailors are."

Grandfather Nat frowned, and nodded. Indeed nobody knew better the common sailor-man's horror of complications and "land-shark" troubles ashore: of anything that might lead to his being asked for responsible evidence, even for his own protection. It gave impunity to three-quarters of the iniquity practised on the high seas.

"An' then o' course he's a deserter," Mr. Cripps proceeded. "So I don't think you'd better say I told you, cap'en—not to him. You can give information—or I can—an' then they'll make him talk, at the Old Bailey; an' they'll bring others."

Grandfather Nat winced, and turned away. Then he stopped again and said angrily: "Damn you, don't meddle! Keep your mouth shut, an' don't meddle."

Mr. Cripps's jaw dropped, and his very nose paled. "But—but——" he stammered, "but, Cap'en, it's murder! Murder agin Beecher an' Vincy too! You'll do something, when it's your own son! Your own son. An' it's murder, Cap'en!"

My grandfather went two steps on his way, with a stifled groan. "Murder!" he muttered, "murder it is, by the law of England!"

Mr. Cripps came at his heels, very blank in the face. Suddenly my grandfather turned on him again, pale and fierce. "Shut your mouth, d'ye hear? Stow your slack jaw, an' mind your own business, or I'll——"

Grandfather Nat lifted his hand; and I believe nothing but a paralysis of terror kept Mr. Cripps from a bolt. Several people stopped to stare, and the old man saw it. So he checked his wrath and walked on.

"I'll see that man," he said presently, flinging the words at Mr. Cripps over his shoulder. And so we reached the Hole in the Wall.

Mr. Cripps sat speechless in the bar and trembled, while Grandfather Nat remained for an hour in the skipper's parlour with Conolly the half-drunken. What they said one to another I never learned, nor even if my grandfather persuaded the man to tell him anything; though there can be no doubt he did.

For myself, I moved uneasily about the bar-parlour, and presently I slipped out into the alley to gaze at the river from the stair-head. I was troubled vaguely, as a child often is who strives to analyse the behaviour of his elders. I stared some while at the barges and the tugs, and at Bill Stagg's boat with its cage of fire, as it went in and about among the shipping; I looked at the bills on the

128

wall, where new tales of men and women Found Drowned displaced those of a week ago; and I fell again into the wonderment and conjecture they always prompted; and last I turned up the alley, though whether to look out on the street or to stop at the bar-parlour door, I had not determined.

As I went, I grew aware of a tall, florid man with thick boots and very large whiskers, who stood at the entry, and regarded me with a wide and ingratiating smile. I had some cloudy remembrance of having seen him before, walking in the street of Wapping Wall; and, as he seemed to be coming to meet me, I went on past the bar-parlour door to meet him.

"Ah!" he said with a slight glance toward the door, "you're a smart fellow, I can see." And he patted my head and stooped. "Now I've got something to show you. See there!"

He pulled a watch from his pocket and opened it. I was much interested to see that the inward part swung clear out from the case, on a hinge, exactly as I had seen happen with another watch on my first evening at the Hole in the Wall. "That's a rum trick, ain't it?" observed the stranger, smiling wider than ever.

I assented, and thanked him for the demonstration.

"Ah," he replied, "you're as clever a lad as ever I see; but I lay you never see a watch like that before?"

"Yes, I did," I answered heartily. "I saw one once."

"No, no," said the florid man, still toying with the watch, "I don't believe that—it's your gammon. Why, where did you see one?"

He shot another stealthy glance toward the bar-parlour door as he said it, and the glance was so unlike the smile that my sleeping caution was alarmed. I remembered how my grandfather had come by the watch with the M on the back; and I remember his repeated warnings that I must not talk.

"——Why, where did you see one?" asked the stranger.

"In a man's hand," I said, with stolid truth.

He looked at me so sharply through his grin that I had an uncomfortable feeling that I had somehow let out the secret after all. But I resolved to hold on tight.

"Ha! ha!" he laughed, "in a man's hand, of course! I knew you was a smart one. Mine hasn't got any letter on the back, you see."

"No," I answered with elaborate indifference; "no letter." And as I spoke I found more matter of surprise. For if I had eyes in my head—and indeed I had sharp ones—there was Mrs. Grimes in a dark entry across the street, watching this grinning questioner and me.

"Some have letters on the back," said the questioner. "Mine ain't that sort. What sort——"

Here Joe the potman dropped, or knocked over, something in the bar-parlour; and the stranger started.

"I think I'm wanted indoors," I said, moving off, glad of the interruption. "Good-bye!"

The florid stranger rose and walked off at once, with a parting smile. He turned at the corner, and went straight away, without so much as a look toward the entry where Mrs. Grimes was. I fancied he walked rather like a policeman.

CHAPTER XXVII
IN THE BAR-PARLOUR

Dan Ogle, blinded and broken, but silent and saving his revenge: Musky Mag, stricken and pitiable, but faithful even if to death: Henry Viney, desperate but fearful, and urgently needy: these three skulked at bay in dark holes by Blue Gate.

Sullen and silent to doggedness, Ogle would give no word to the hospital doctors of how his injury had befallen; and in three days he would brook confinement no longer, but rose and broke away, defiant of persuasion, to grope into the outer world by aid of Mag's arm. Blind George was about still, but had scarcely been near the Highway except at night, when, as he had been wont to boast, he was as good as most men with sound eyes. It was thought that he spent his days over the water, as would be the way of one feeling the need of temporary caution. It did not matter: that could rest a bit. Blind George should be paid, and paid bitter measure; but first the job in hand, first the scheme he had interrupted; first the money.

Here were doubt and difficulty. Dan Ogle's plan of murder and comprehensive pillage was gone by the board; he was next to helpless. It was plain that, whatever plan was followed, Viney must bear the active part; Dan Ogle raved and cursed to find his partner so unpractised a ruffian, so cautious and doubtful a confederate.

Mrs. Grimes made the matter harder, and it was plain that the thing must be either brought to a head or wholly abandoned, if only on her account. For she had her own idea, with her certain revenge on Captain Nat, and a contingent reward; furthermore, she saw her brother useless. And things were brought to a head when she would wait no more, but carried her intrigue to the police.

Nothing but a sudden move would do now, desperate as it might be; and the fact screwed Viney to the sticking-place, and gave new vigour to Ogle's shaken frame. After all, the delay had not been great—no more than a few days. Captain Nat suspected nothing, and the chances lay that the notes were still in hand, as they had been when Ogle's sister last saw them; for he could afford to hold them, and dispose of them at a later and safer time. The one danger was from this manœuvre of Mrs. Grimes: if the police thought well enough of her tale to act without preliminary inquiry, they might be at the Hole in the Wall with a search-warrant at any moment. The thing must be done at once—that very night.

Musky Mag had never left Dan's side a moment since she had brought him from the hospital; now she was thrust aside, and bidden to keep to herself. Viney took to pen, ink and paper; and the two men waited impatiently for midnight.

It was then that Viney, with Ogle at his elbow, awaited the closing of the Hole in the Wall, hidden in the dark entry, whence Mrs. Grimes had watched the plain-clothes policeman fishing for information a few hours earlier. The customers grew noisier as the hour neared; and Captain Nat's voice was heard enjoining order once or twice, ere at last it was raised to clear the bar. Then the company came out, straggling and staggering, wrangling and singing, and melted away into the dark, this way and that. Mr. Cripps went east, the pale pensioner west, each like a man who has all night to get home in; and the potman, having fastened the shutters, took his coat and hat, and went his way also.

There was but one other tavern in sight, and that closed at the same time as the Hole in the Wall; and since none nearer than Paddy's Goose remained open till one, Wapping Wall was soon dark and empty. There were diamond-shaped holes near the top of the shutters at the Hole in the Wall, and light was visible through these: a sign that Captain Nat was still engaged in the bar. Presently the light dulled, and then disappeared: he had extinguished the lamps. Now was the time—while he was in the bar-parlour. Viney came out from the entry, pulling Ogle by the arm, and crossed the street. He brought him to the court entrance, and placed his hand on the end post.

"This is the first post in the court," Viney whispered. "Wait here while I go. We both know what's to do."

Viney tip-toed to the bar-parlour door, and tapped. There was a heavy footstep within, and the door was flung open. There stood

131

Captain Nat with the table-lamp in his hand. "Who's that?" said Captain Nat. "Come into the light."

Viney took a deep breath. "Me," he answered. "I'll come in; I've got something to say."

He went in side-foremost, with his back against the door-post, and Captain Nat turned slowly, each man watching the other. Then the landlord put the lamp on the table, and shut the door. "Well," he said, "I'll hear you say it."

There was something odd about Captain Nat's eyes: something new, and something that Viney did not like. Hard and quiet; not anger, it would seem, but some-thing indefinable—and worse. Viney braced himself with another inspiration of breath.

"First," he said, "I'm alone here, but I've left word. There's a friend o' mine not far off, waiting. He's waiting where he can hear the clock strike on Shadwell Church, just as you can hear it here; an' if I'm not back with him, safe an' sound, when it strikes one, he's going to the police with some papers I've given him, in an envelope."

"Ah! An' what papers?"

"Papers I've written myself. Papers with a sort of private log in them—not much like the one they showed 'em at Lloyd's—of the loss of the Florence years enough ago, when a man named Dan Webb was killed. Papers with the names of most of the men aboard, an' hints as to where to find some of 'em: Bill Stagg, for instance, A. B. They may not want to talk, but they can be made."

Captain Nat's fixed look was oddly impassive. "Have you got it on the papers," he said, in a curiously even voice, as though he recited a lesson learned by rote; "have you got it on the papers that Dan Webb had got at the rum, an' was lost through bein' drunk?"

"No, I haven't; an' much good it 'ud do ye if I had. Drunk or sober he died in that wreck, an' not a man aboard but knew all about that. I've told you, before, what it is by law: Murder. Murder an' the Rope."

"Ay," said Captain Nat in the same even voice, though the tones grew in significance as he went on. "Ay, you have; an' you made me pay for the information. Murder it is, an' the Rope, by the law of England."

"Well, I want none of your money now; I want my own. I'll go back an' burn those papers—or give 'em to you, if you like—an' you'll never see me again, if you'll do one thing—not with your money."

"What?"

"Give me my partner's leather pocket-book and my eight hundred and ten pounds that was in it. That's first an' last of my business here to-night, an' all I've got to say."

132

For a moment Captain Nat's impassibility was disturbed, and he looked sharply at Viney. "Ha!" he said, "what's this? Partner's pocket-book? Notes? What?"

"I've said it plain, an' you understand me. Time's passing, Cap'en Kemp, an' you'd better not waste it arguing; one o'clock'll strike before long. The money I came an' spoke about when they found Marr in the river; you had it all the time, an' you knew it. That's what I want: nothing o' yours, but my own money. Give me my own money, an' save your neck."

Captain Nat compressed his lips, and folded his arms. "There was a woman knew about this," he said slowly, after a pause, "a woman an' a man. They each took a try at that money, in different ways. They must be friends o' yours."

"Time's going, Cap'en Kemp, time's going! Listen to reason, an' give me what's my own. I want nothing o' yours; nothing but my own. To save you; and—and that boy. You've got a boy to remember: think o' the boy!"

Captain Nat stood for a little, silent and thoughtful, his eyes directed absently on Viney, as though he saw him not; and as he stood so the darkness cleared from his face. Not that moment's darkness only, but all the hardness of years seemed to abate in the old skipper's features, so that presently Captain Nat stood transfigured.

"Ay," he said at last, "the boy—I'll think o' the boy, God bless him! You shall have your money, Viney: though whether it ought to be yours I don't know. Viney, when you came in I was ready to break you in pieces with my bare hands—which I could do easy, as you know well enough." He stretched forth the great knotted hands, and Viney shrank before them. "I was ready to kill you with my hands, an' would ha' done it, for a reason I'll tell you of, afterwards. But I've done evil enough, an' I'll do no more. You shall have your money. Wait here, an' I'll fetch it."

"Now, no—no tricks, you know!" said Viney, a little nervously, as the old man turned toward the staircase door.

"Tricks?" came the answer. "No. An end of all tricks." And Captain Nat tramped heavily up the stair.

CHAPTER XXVIII
STEPHEN'S TALE

My grandfather was uncommonly silent all that day, after his interview with Conolly. He bade me good night when I went to bed, and kissed me; but he said no more, though he sat by my bed till I fell asleep, while Joe attended the bar.

I had a way, now and again, of waking when the bar was closed—perhaps because of the noise; and commonly at these times I lay awake till Grandfather Nat came to bed, to bid him good night once more. It was so this night, the night of nights. I woke at the shouting and the stumbling into the street, and lay while the bar was cleared, and the doors banged and fastened.

My grandfather seemed to stay uncommonly long; and presently, as the night grew stiller, I was aware of voices joined in conversation below. I wondered greatly who could be talking with Grandfather Nat at this hour, and I got out of bed to listen at the stair-head. It could not be Bill Stagg, for the voices were in the bar-parlour, and not in the store-place behind; and it was not Joe the potman, for I had heard him go, and I knew his step well. I wondered if Grandfather Nat would mind if I went down to see.

I was doubtful, and I temporised; I began to put on some clothes, listening from time to time at the stair-head, in hope that I might recognise the other voice. But indeed both voices were indistinct, and I could not distinguish one from the other. And then of a sudden the stairfoot door opened, and my grandfather came upstairs, heavy and slow.

I doubted what he might say when he saw my clothes on, but he seemed not to notice it. He brought a candle in from the landing, and he looked strangely grave—grave with a curious composure. He went to the little wall-cupboard at his bed-head, and took out the cash-box, which had not been downstairs since the pale man had ceased work. "Stevy, my boy," he said, "have you said your prayers?"

"Yes, grandfather."

"An' didn't forget Gran'father Nat?"

"No, grandfather, I never forget you."

"Good boy, Stevy." He took the leather pocket-book from the box, and knelt by my side, with his arm about me. "Stevy," he said, "here's this money. It ain't ours, Stevy, neither yours nor mine, an' we've no right to it. I kept it for you, but I did wrong; an' worse, I was leadin' you wrong. Will you give it up, Stevy?"

"Why, yes, grandfather." Truly that was an easy enough thing to say; and in fact I was in some way pleased to know that my mother had been right, after all.

"Right, Stevy; be an honest boy always, and an honest man—better than me. Since I was a boy like you, I've gone a long way wrong, an' I've been a bad man, Stevy, a bad man some ways, at least. An' now, Stevy, I'm goin' away—for a bit. Presently, when I'm gone, you can go to the stairs an' call Bill Stagg—he'll come at once. Call Bill Stagg—he'll stay with you to-night. You don't mind Bill Stagg, do you?"

Bill Stagg was an excellent friend of mine, and I liked his company; but I could not understand Grandfather Nat's going away. Where was he going, and why, so late at night?

"Never mind that just now, Stevy. I'm going away—for a bit; an' whatever happens you'll always say prayers night an' mornin' for Gran'father Nat, won't you? An' be a good boy."

There was something piteous now in my grandfather's hard, grave face. "Don't go, grandfather," I pleaded, with my arm at his neck, "don't go! Grandfather Nat! You're not—not going to die, are you?"

"That's as God wills, my boy. We must all die some day."

I think he was near breaking down here; but at the moment a voice called up the stairs.

"Are you coming?" said the voice. "Time's nearly up!" And it frightened me more than I can say to know this second voice at last for Viney's.

But my grandfather was firm again at once. "Yes," he cried, "I'm coming!... No more to do, Stevy—snivelling's no good." And then Grandfather Nat put his hands clumsily together, and shut his eyes like a little child. "God bless an' save this boy, whatever happens. Amen," said Grandfather Nat.

Then he rose and took from the cash-box the watch that the broken-nosed man had sold. "There's that, too," he said musingly. "I dunno why I kep' it so long." And with that he shut the cash-box, and strode across to the landing. He looked back at me for a moment, but said nothing; and then descended the stairs.

Bewildered and miserably frightened, I followed him.

I could neither reason nor cry out, and I had an agonised hope that I was not really awake, and that this was just such a nightmare as had afflicted me on the night of the murder at our door. I crouched on the lower stairs, and listened....

135

"Yes, I've got it," said my grandfather, answering an eager question. "There it is. Look at that—count the notes."

I heard a hasty scrabbling of paper.

"Right?" asked my grandfather.

"Quite right," Viney answered; and there was exultation in his voice.

"Pack 'em up—put 'em safe in your pocket. Quite safe? There's the watch, too; I paid for that."

"Oh, the watch? Well, all right, I don't mind having that too, since you're pressing.... You might ha' saved a deal of trouble, yours an' mine too, if you'd done all this before."

"Yes, you're right; but I clear up all now. You've got the notes all quite safe, have you?"

"All safe." There was the sound of a slap on a breast-pocket.

"And the watch?"

"Ay; and the watch."

"Good!..."

I heard a bounce and a gasp of terror; and then my grandfather's voice again. "Come! Come, Viney! We'll be quits to the end. We're bad men both, an' we'll go to the police together. Bring your papers, Viney! Tell 'em about the Florence an' Dan Webb, an' I'll tell 'em about the Juno an' my boy! I've got my witnesses—an' I'll find more—a dozen to your one! Come, Viney! I'll have justice done now, on both of us!"

I could stay no longer. Viney was struggling desperately, reasoning, entreating. I pushed open the staircase door, but neither seemed to note me. My grandfather had Viney by arm and collar, and was shaking him, face downward.

"I'll go halves, Kemp—I'll go halves," Viney gasped hoarsely. "Divide how you like—but don't, don't be a fool! Take five hundred! Think o' the boy!"

"I've thought of the boy, an' I've thought of his father! God'll mind the boy you've made an orphan! Come!"

My grandfather flung wide the door, and tumbled Viney up the steps into the court. The little table with the lamp on it rocked from a kick, and I saved it by sheer instinct, for I was sick with terror.

I followed into the court, and saw my grandfather now nearly at the street corner, hustling and dragging his prisoner. "Dan! Dan!" Viney was crying, struggling wildly. "Dan! I've got it! Draw him off me, Dan! Go for the kid an' draw him off! Go for the kid on the stairs!"

And I could see a man come groping between the wall and the

136

posts, a hand feeling from one post to the next, and the stick in the other hand scraping the wall. I ran out to the farther side of the alley.

Viney's shout distracted my grandfather's attention, and I saw him looking anxiously back. With that Viney took his chance, and flung himself desperately round the end post. His collar went with a rip, and he ran. For a moment my grandfather stood irresolute, and I ran toward him. "I am safe here," I cried. "Come away, grandfather!"

But when he saw me clear of the groping man, he turned and dashed after Viney; while from the bar-parlour I heard a curse and a crash of broken glass. I vaguely wondered if Viney's confederate were smashing windows in the partition; and then I ran my hardest after Grandfather Nat.

Viney had made up the street toward the bridge and Ratcliff Highway, and Captain Nat pursued with shouts of "Stop him!" Breathless and unsteady, I made slow progress with my smaller legs over the rough cobble-stones, which twisted my feet all ways as I ran. But I was conscious of a gathering of other cries ahead, and I struggled on, with throbbing head and bursting heart. Plainly there were more shouts as I neared the corner, and a running of more men than two. And when the corner was turned, and the bridge and the lock before me, I saw that the chase was over.

Three bull's-eye lanterns were flashing to and fro, pointing their long rays down on the black dock-water, and the policemen who directed them were calling to dockmen on the dark quay, who cried back, and ran, and called again.

"Man in!" cried one and another, hurrying in from the Highway. "Fell off the lock." "No, he cut his lucky, an' headered in!" "He didn't, I tell ye!" "Yes, he did! Why, I see 'im!"

I could not see my grandfather; and for a moment my thumping heart stood still and sick with the fear that it was he who was drowning in the dock. Then a policeman swung his lantern across to the opposite side, and in the passing flash Grandfather Nat's figure stood hard and clear for an instant and no more. He was standing midway on the lock, staring and panting, and leaning on a stanchion.

With a dozen risks of being knocked into the dock by excited onlookers, I scrambled down to the lock and seized the first stanchion. It creaked and tottered in my hand, but I went forward, gripping at the swaying chain and keeping foothold on the slippery, uneven timbers I knew not how. Sometimes the sagging chain would give till I felt myself pitching headlong, only to be saved by the check of the stanchion against the side of the socket; and once the chain hung so low, where it had slipped through the next stanchion-eye, that I had no choice but to let go, and plunged in the dark for the next upright—it might have been to plunge into space. "Grandfather Nat! Grandfather Nat!"

I reached him somehow at last, and caught tight at his wrist. He was leaning on the stanchion still, and staring at the dark water. "Here I am, grandfather," I said, "but I am frightened. Stay with me, please!"

For a little while he still peered into the gloom. Then he turned and said quietly: "I've lost him, Stevy. He went over—here."

By the sweep of his hand I saw what had happened, though I could scarce realise the whole matter then and there. As I presently learnt, however, Viney was running full for the bridge, with Captain Nat shouting behind him, when he saw the lanterns of the three policemen barring the bridge as they came on their beat from the Highway. To avoid them he swung aside and made for the lock, with his pursuer hard at his heels. Now a lock of that sort joins in an angle or mitre at the middle, where the two sides meet like a valve, pointing to resist the tide; so that the hazardous path along the top turns off sharply midway. Flying headlong, with thought of nothing but the avenger behind him, Viney overran the angle, meeting the low chain full under his knees; and so was gone, with a yell and a splash.

Grandfather Nat took me by the collar, and turned me round. "We'll get back, Stevy," he said. "Go on, I'll hold you tight."

And so in the pitchy dark I went back along the way I had come, walking before my grandfather as I had done when first I saw that lock. The dockmen had flung random life-buoys, and now were groping with drags and hooks. Some judged that the man must have gone under like a stone; others thought it quite likely that a good swimmer might have got away quietly. And everybody wished to know who the man was, and why he was running.

To all such questions my grandfather made the same answer. "It was a man I wanted, wanted bad, for the police. You find him, dead or alive, an' I'll identify him, an' say the rest in the proper place; that's all." Only once he amplified this answer, and then he said: "You can judge he was as much afraid o' the police as he was o' me, or more. Look where he went, when he saw 'em on the bridge!" And again he repeated: "I'll say the rest when he's found, not before; an' nobody can make me."

He was calm and cool enough now, as I could feel as well as hear, for my hand was buried in his, while he pushed his way

138

stolidly through the little crowd. As for myself, I could neither think, nor speak, nor laugh, nor cry, though dizzily conscious of an impulse to do all four at once. I had Grandfather Nat again, and now he would not go away; that I could realise; and I clung with all my might to as much of his hand as I could grip.

CHAPTER XXIX
STEPHEN'S TALE

But I was to have neither time to gather my wits nor quiet to assort my emotions: for the full issue of that night was not yet. Even as we were pushing through the little crowd, and even as my grandfather parried question with answer, a new cry rose, and at the sound the crowd began to melt: for it was the cry of "Fire."

A single shout at first, and then another, and then a clamour of three together, and a beat of running feet. Men about us started off, and as we rounded the corner, one came running back on his tracks. "Cap'en Kemp, it's your house!" he cried. "Your house, Cap'en Kemp! The Hole in the Wall! The Hole in the Wall!"

Then was dire confusion. I was caught in a whir of running men, and I galloped and stumbled along as I might, dragging dependent from my grandfather's hand. Somewhere ahead a wavering light danced before my eyes, and there was a sudden outburst of loud cracks, as of a hundred carters' whips; and then— screams; screams without a doubt. Confusedly my mind went back to Viney's confederate, groping in at the bar-parlour door. What had he done? Smashed glass? Glass? It must have been the lamp: the lamp on the little table by the door, the lamp I had myself saved but ten minutes earlier!

Now we were opposite the Hole in the Wall, and the loud cracks were joined with a roar of flame. Out it came gushing at the crevices of doors and shutters, and the corners of doors and shutters shrivelled and curled to let out more, as though that bulging old wooden house were a bursting reservoir of long-pent fire that could be held in no more. And still there were the screams, hoarser and hoarser, from what part within was not to be guessed.

My grandfather stood me in a doorway, up two steps, and ran toward the court, but that was impassable. With such fearful swiftness had the fire sprung up and over the dry old timber on this

139

side, where it had made its beginning, that already a painted board on the brick wall opposite was black and smoking and glowering red at the edges; and where I stood, across the road, the air was hot and painful to the eyes. Grandfather Nat ran along the front of the house to the main door, but it was blazing and bursting, and he turned and ran into the road, with his arm across his eyes. Then, with a suddenly increased roar, flames burst tenfold in volume and number from all the ground floor, and, where a shutter fell, all within glowed a sheer red furnace. The spirit was caught at last.

And now I saw a sight that would come again in sleep months afterwards, and set me screaming in my bed. The cries, which had lately died down, sprang out anew amid the roar, nearer and clearer, with a keener agony; and up in the club-room, the room of the inquests—there at a window appeared the Groping Man, a dreadful figure. In no darkness now, but ringed about with bright flame I saw him: the man whose empty, sightless eye-pits I had seen scarce twelve hours before through a hole in a canvas screen. The shade was gone from over the place of the eyes, and down the seared face and among the rags of blistered skin rolled streams of horrible great tears, forced from the raw lids by scorching smoke. His clothes smoked about him as he stood—groping, groping still, he knew not whither; and his mouth opened and closed with sounds scarce human.

Grandfather Nat roared distractedly for a ladder, called to the man to jump, ran forward twice to the face of the house as though to catch him, and twice came staggering back with his hands over his face, and flying embers singeing his hair and his coat.

The blind man's blackened hands came down on the blazing sill, and leapt from the touch. Then came a great crash, with a single second's dulling of the whole blaze. For an instant the screaming, sightless, weeping face remained, and then was gone for ever. The floor had fallen.

The flames went up with a redoubled roar, and now I could hold my place no longer for the heat. People were flinging water over the shutters and doors of the houses facing the fire, and from the houses adjoining furniture was being dragged in hot haste. My grandfather came and carried me a few doors farther along the street, and left me with a chandler's wife, who was out in a shawl and a man's overcoat over a huddle of flannel petticoats.

Now the fire engines came, dashing through the narrow lanes with a clamour of hoarse cries, and scattering the crowd this way and that. The Hole in the Wall was past aid, and all the work was given to save its neighbours. For some while I could distinguish my

140

grandfather among the firemen, heaving and hauling, and doing the work of three. The police were grown in numbers now, and they had cleared the street to beyond where I stood, so that I could see well enough; and in every break in the flames, in every changing shadow, I saw again the face of the Groping Man, even as I can see it now as I write.

Floor went upon floor, till at last the poor old shell fell in a heap amid a roar of shouts and a last leap of fire, leaving the brick wall of the next house cracking and black and smoking, and tagged with specks of dying flame. And then at last my grandfather, black and scorched, came and sat by me on a step, and put the breast of his coat about me.

And that was the end of the Hole in the Wall: the end of its landlord's doubts and embarrassments and dangers, and the beginning of another chapter in his history—his history and mine.

CHAPTER XXX
STEPHEN'S TALE

Little remains to say; for with the smoking sticks of the Hole in the Wall the tale of my early days burns itself out.

Viney's body was either never found or never identified. Whether it was discovered by some person who flung it adrift after possessing himself of the notes and watch: whether it was held unto dissolution by mud, or chains, or waterside gear: or whether indeed, as was scarce possible, it escaped with the life in it, to walk the world in some place that knew it not, I, at any rate, cannot tell. The fate of his confederate, at least, was no matter of doubt. He must have been driven to the bar by the fire he had raised, and there, bewildered and helpless, and cut off from the way he had come, even if he could find it, he must have scrambled desperately till he found the one open exit—the club-room stairs.

But of these enough. Faint by contrast with the vivid scenes of the night, divers disconnected impressions of the next morning remain with me: all the fainter for the sleep that clutched at my eyelids, spite of my anxious resolution to see all to the very end. Of a coarse, draggled woman of streaming face and exceeding bitter cry, who sat inconsolable while men raked the ruins for a thing

141

unrecognisable when it was found. Of the pale man, who came staring and choking, and paler than ever, gasping piteously of his long and honest service, and sitting down on the curb at last, to meditate on my grandfather's promise that he should not want, if he would work. And of Mr. Cripps, at first blank and speechless, and then mighty loquacious in the matter of insurance. For works of art would be included, of course, up to twenty pounds apiece; at which amount of proceeds—with a discount to Captain Kemp—he would cheerfully undertake to replace the lot, and throw the signboard in.

Mrs. Grimes was heard of, though not seen; but this was later. She was long understood to have some bitter grievance against the police, whom she charged with plots and conspiracies to defeat the ends of justice; and I think she ended with a savage assault on a plain-clothes constable's very large whiskers, and twenty-one days' imprisonment.

The Hole in the Wall was rebuilt in brick, with another name, as I think you may see it still; or could, till lately. There was also another landlord. For Captain Nat Kemp turned to enlarging and improving his wharf, and he bought lighters, and Wapping saw him no more. As for me, I went to school at last.

142

Lightning Source UK Ltd.
Milton Keynes UK
UKHW041856270422
402077UK00002B/3/J

9 781647 999186